To Ryan:

DEATH HIGHWAY

The Red Plane feeds on the mundane!

Great to meet you in person!

J.C.W

DEATH HIGHWAY

J.C. Walsh

Death Highway

By J.C. Walsh

Edited by Jenny Adams

Copyright © 2019 by J.C. Walsh

All rights reserved. No part of this publication may be reproduced, or transmitted in any form or by any means, electronic or otherwise, without written permission from the author.

This is a work of fiction. Any semblance to actual persons living or dead, business, events, or locales is purely coincidental. The author has taken great liberties with locales including the creation of fictional towns.

Reproduction in whole or part of this publication without express written consent is strictly prohibited.

Cover © 2019 by Allison Carmichael.

SPECIAL THANKS

I would like to thank my wife Colleen for the amazing support through this wild journey. To my friends and family, especially my parents for encouraging my creativity and always believing in me. To Armand Rosamilia for being an inspiring mentor and pushing me to finally get my first book released. To Chuck Buda, Tim Meyer, Frank Edler, and Todd Keisling for their friendship and support. To my brother, for being the sole inspiration of the main character so many years ago. And to you, the Reader, thank you for taking a ride on Death Highway. I hope you leave the same way you've entered.

PART ONE

THE RED PLANE

1.

This is how the world ends. With me stuck inside a cell, unable to see beyond these walls as I feel every cut, every little slice of death inflicted. The worst thing about doing time is not the time itself, but what's transpiring inside of me. I am helpless, forced to fight the madness spreading from the bleeding wounds. It all started with the accident, the day my best friend's car exploded in my face. The Universe spoke.

Its irregular breathing was an ominous sigh echoing through my ears. I felt its hot breath in the ambulance. Then again as I lay in my hospital bed, close to dying from the severity of the burns. The doctors later said it was a miracle they were able to save me.

My family was there. I couldn't see them, not at first. At first, I thought they were an illusion shimmering over me. The veil over my eyes eventually lifted; it could've been minutes later, hours, hell even days. Time did not exist when all I did was lay still, nerves screaming in pain, trying to burrow through and exit my burnt flesh. My right side, afflicted by third degree burns, was bandaged up from the leg, to my face, and my head. I must've been there for some time; the bandages had gone from white to a yellowish red. My new friend was the click of a button, my body welcomed the morphine as it entered my body. My head was a chart, what's your pain level? Well, since you asked, it was a super ten, now it's a six. I counted the seconds before the next escalation.

Laura's face hovered over me, plastered to the slow ticking of time, tears frozen on her face. She was on my left side while my Grandparents stood by me on the right. I didn't want them anywhere near those bandages. I didn't want what was burrowing through to burn them with its pain. All their faces were grave, I was buried inside. Was I dead? Or was I between the world of the living and the dead? The flesh of our world was peeling away red; I don't know how I know this, but I do. The accident. I remembered the accident.

Then came the healing. The whole process was a blur of agony. Days of skin grafts and scrubbing to keep the wounds clean, to keep me clear of infection even though I knew I was already infected inside. Days were spent watching myself peel away, becoming the new me underneath. A monster.

The doctors did what they could, but the damage was bad. The patchwork of scars mapping the right side of my body made me think of small twisted roots of a tree. Those areas of my body are so tight it's hard to move. They told me physical therapy and stretches would help loosen up the flesh, make mobility easier. More days spent in a blur. It's the veil I don't want to lift, to relive those moments of pure torture. The memory makes me grit my teeth, my pain level says hello at an eight.

Why am I thinking of all this now?

It's almost time.

My mind becomes a racket ball of chaotic imagery. Memories. I am an outsider to these memories, unable to piece them together properly because I am watching someone else's life play out, someone that looks like me. I can't hold onto one damn image to see if it's real or not. When I think I grasp it, the memory disappears in a wisp of smoke between my scarred fingers.

Ants. That's what the scars feel like years later. It's never one ant crawling along those areas. It would be so easy to flick the little sucker, send him flying on his way. No. It's a fucking congregation. A cluster fuck of ants that begin their onslaught in one spot. The itching and burning turns to pain. Pain level starts at a four. I can't help but focus on it, how it momentarily stays in that one spot, a dull achiness. Then it spreads throughout other scars. Pain level four becomes a six, then an eight. The needle is way past ten and I'm in the red, baby; I'm ready to murder someone.

"Don't tell me you're there again." Jesse says from the bottom bunk.

"Where?" I'm staring at the ceiling. No pictures of loved ones to help me get through my years of being incarcerated. It's blank for a reason. I don't trust those pictures, the stories behind them, I don't want them inside of my brain while I search for the truth of who I am. What I am.

"You're thinking too much."

Jesse has been my cellmate ever since I became a resident of The Rhode Island Correctional Institute. I tell Jesse everything; he's the closest thing I have to a friend.

"Weird dreams again," I reply.

"Your red place?"

"Red Plane."

"Same thing isn't it?"

"I don't know."

"Few days left, buddy. You're out of here. Don't get lost on me now."

He's right. My sentence is nearly up, must be the reason I've been thinking about the accident lately. During my two year stay, I kept my head down the entire sentence, stayed out of trouble the best I could, behaved like a good boy. Sure, there were scuffles here and there. Nothing serious. Thankfully the board of corrections didn't let the small fights stain my reputation. I'm lucky they recognized, with each conflict, I was defending myself and not the instigator. I never lost my temper, I kept my attitude at bay, and I did what the programs insist. I was a model prisoner. I was saved!

The world exhales another death rattle. I will be released into a dying world.

I'm not confident I can save it.

When I first arrived, I was still a timid animal. Afraid, yet my eyes stayed focused and not wild. I didn't trust the many faces watching me from their cells. I felt like weak prey waiting for the cages to open, for the predators inside to pounce on me once they were let free. Jesse had saved me. Brought me out of myself, from the animal that knew nothing but to bare its teeth. I did it to my family and friends when they did their best to support me; I'll do it to anyone else dare that dares get in my path.

I didn't want to talk to Jesse when I had first entered my cell. I stared down at his smiling face as he lay on the bottom bunk. From what I had heard, inmates didn't like taking the top bunk, whether because they were the new guy, or because the current one didn't trust the new guy. Defiant by nature, I had taken the top bunk.

But, instead of getting shanked early on, I learned quickly of his positive and happy demeanor; it slowly relaxed me. He loved to talk a lot, maybe too much. Then again, I didn't talk enough, someone had to fill the dead space. His outgoing personality had given me something to focus on in the early weeks of my sentence. It was a pleasant distraction instead of trying to see through that blank ceiling, into the Red Plane, trying to piece together my mind, and rid myself of the gnawing pain deep inside my flesh.

Come to find out, Jesse is a free-spirited speed junkie with a fond love of muscle cars, much like myself. We talked about the thrill of driving fast, defying the mundane world and its laws, with the roar of the engine, and the world whipping by on both sides. True freedom. Talking with him in the early days had brought a happiness that I thought had died with the other half of me, but it also filled me with sadness. I'm not free anymore; I am part of something the mundane world shuns more than driving fast cars.

We also share the common love for the bottle. Jesse was a drinker, his other addiction. Put two and two together, and its pure disaster.

"While you were street racing against the grim reaper, Randy, I was driving with him in my lap. The grim reaper was my road soda. It landed me in jail many times. Finally, my luck ran out and I hit someone. Here I am."

"The worst thing is," he said, "even though the guy is paralyzed from the waist down, he didn't press charges."

"How's that the worst thing?" I asked.

"Well, if that was me paralyzed, I'd fuck up his entire life, make sure I got revenge on the person who had put me in that wheelchair. But he wasn't like that. Maybe it was because he was coming out of a bar when I hit him, maybe he had also had a few to drink. I don't know. I won't rat on him, either. To be honest, I think they forget to check his blood alcohol the moment they found the open bottle of vodka in the car."

I cringed. "Vodka?"

He ignored me and continued his story.

He said it had happened so fast he had no idea what he had hit. All he saw was something white and round hit the windshield, and the other object that bounced off the front of his car was the size of a small horse. He looked in the rearview mirror to find, to his dismay, a human body unmoving in the middle of the intersection, his motorcycle a wreck of metal nearby. Pieces of both Jesse's car and the guy's motorcycle were scattered all over the street. Within minutes, the place was an array of colors from the lights of firetrucks, police, and ambulance. The intersection looked like a mini war zone.

"The funny thing is, my car was still drivable. I thought about jumping back in and getting the hell out of there. But I couldn't leave the guy like that. I knew it would haunt me for the rest of my life. I ran to the middle of the intersection, my cell phone was out, and my thumbs moved over the numbers to dial 911; at the same time, I watched the guy's chest to make sure he was breathing. A cop pulled up. Ironic, he was at a Dunkin Donuts nearby and had seen everything while he had his car parked in the lot, having a coffee, and, yes, you guessed it, a donut." Jesse laughed, "He was a nice guy. Even when he discovered my passenger, he calmly asked me how much I had of that bottle. And, well, here I am. What's your story?"

   I kept it short and sweet. I was starting to like him, appreciated his story. Wasn't ready to fully tell mine. So, I told him I was street racing in an old industrial area. Before I knew it, I had lost control of the car and collided with the other racer. His car caught on fire; I tried to help. I was on fire and there was an explosion. I blacked out and woke up in the burn unit. Once I was healed and had done the physical therapy, a clean bill of health was pushed. The state couldn't wait; they wanted my ass in the can. The state of Rhode Island was sick and tired of street racing plaguing their city. Once I was ready to stand trial, the court was able to sentence me for two years for a misdemeanor for the street racing and accidental manslaughter, since someone had died during the race.

   So, Jesse and I had become good friends. For two years we had shared the same cell, we shared the same interests, and, as luck would have it, we both worked in the automotive work shop in the prison. I saw it as luck, but Jesse saw it as fate. Despite everything I had been through, and the strange cosmic feeling rattling inside of me, I was still skeptical of the concept of fate. Within time, I began to see what he did. Still, on those days we have our talks, I'm glad to occupy the top bunk, while he speaks his positive wisdom from the bottom. He will never see the smile on my face when I think about what hope could mean. Nor will he see the haunted look in my eyes, betraying my smile. I don't see redemption. I see red. I don't think I am seeking it, either. Once I am out of this place, I seek the road to damnation, and only then, may I find redemption.

I feel the sharpened end of a tooth brush.

A fucking tooth brush, stabbing me in the neck over and over, spraying my blank ceiling with my blood. I don't see the face; it's shielded in a swirling blackness. I release my last breath, close my eyes. Wait for death. When it doesn't come for me, I open my eyes to find I am alive, right in the middle of our usual ritual of conversations, and laughter. It's like we were never interrupted.

So, yeah, it's hard to trust what my mind shows me.

It's not the first time the memory of my death had snaked its way into my thoughts, slithered into my dreams. Each time I woke from it, my neck hurt, and I tasted blood for a week.

The ceiling is blank.

I need to get out. I need to go to Death Highway.

The next day I am anxious from the moment I wake up. As the Correction Officer leads us through the mazes of cells, the noises from other inmates sound like mourning doves with brain damage. Their voices are jarring. Not even a cup of coffee can help the overwhelming feeling. You're almost there, I tell myself. Don't lose it now. Keep your head down, stay in line and get to work. Once we enter the work shop, I inhale deeply. Anxiety withers, pain level is dense. Purpose. Even if it's just a few more days, I need this now more than ever.

Under supervision at a distance, the guards keep a watchful eye. Inmates mostly work on prison transports, but there's the occasional muscle car that one lucky bastard can get his hands on. One of the inmates, who got his name because he used to be a bartender, Frosted Billy, gets to work on one of those cars, an old 1970 Ford Mustang, if my memory serves me right. A thing of beauty. Not going to lie, I'm a little envious. But sometimes just doing the work because it needs to be done is more satisfying than doing it just for fun. Jesse assists as we remove the rotors from an old transport bus, and then I go to town scraping away at the rust. This relaxes me; I feel like I am scraping away at my anxiety and I bringing my mind back into focus. Cleaning all four rotors and replacing the brakes takes a good part of the day.

A man is most powerful when he can use his hands.

The words bring glimpses of happier times, words that my Grandpa used. They cut through the fog of memory, keeping my head clear while I continue my path. I see the small boy I once was, standing on the step ladder, carefully bending over the front of the car to peak underneath the hood, watching Grandpa perform a tune up on the engine of our neighbor's car. Sometimes he'd point at a part and then test me to see if I remembered what it was; other times he'd be very quiet while he worked, face stone-like with concentration, as the wrench rhythmically clicked back and forth.

I remember how strong he was. When I reached the age of twelve, the engine lift wasn't working right. So being the tough guy he was, Grandpa decided to pull out the engine himself like it was nothing. Our good family friend, John Slater, was there. He couldn't believe his eyes as he watched this man in his late fifties do something like that. Once he snapped out of it, he assisted Grandpa getting the engine block secured and tightly strapped onto the lift. John called him a crazy bastard.

"All right, inmates." The Correction Officer's voice brings me out of my memories, "We are done for the day."

Jesse stands next to me while our fellow co-workers, all good guys I'm going to miss when I leave, start to file out. Jesse gets in line, I'm right behind him when the guard steps between us, stopping me.

"Not you, Jones." His hand comes up, nearly striking me in the chest. His voice sounds more authoritative than usual.

"What's up, Dave?"

By now I know the officers by name. I had never really had a problem with any of them before, even the ones who occasionally liked to stretch the wings of their authority. Dave was hardly ever like that; he was always friendly, cooperative and just let us inmates do our work. If someone was out of line, then Dave did what his job required of him. If that led to him getting a little rough on one of the guys, who was I to judge? This is different.

"Evaluation." He answers curtly.

Another officer starts pushing Jesse out the door, the confusion on his face matches my own. My thoughts are clanging around in my head, everything is cloudy. I don't even remember the other officer's name. Just Dave. Dave with his hand still inches from my chest, his jaw tight.

"Now?" I ask, trying to watch my tone, "Here?"

"Yup, someone will be with you in a moment." he says. Dave takes a few steps back, the tense look is now grave, apologetic. He steps out of the shop; the sound of steel slamming shut is louder than it should be. The lock clicks into place.

I don't trust the silence, it's oppressive. I get the feeling I am not alone.

Footsteps sound from the back of the shop. A socket skitters across the floor from someone kicking it, hands slap on the hoods of cars. Maniacal laughter fills the empty space. They draw closer. I can feel their shadows upon me; I slowly turn to face my company.

There're at least eight guys, all with shaved heads. Their shirtless bodies reveal the tapestry of tattoos decorating their skin. The imagery is arcane and ritualistic, spiced with an apocalyptic scene of men suffering to gods and monsters. The most recognizable of them all is one symbol, the swastika. Nazis. Not just your typical Nazis either. I've heard of these guys, seen them lurking around the prison yard while I'm weight training. Nazi Occultists. I have a bad feeling I may know why they are here.

I pull off the top of my uniform, only a muscle shirt underneath, showing off my own muscular body, not to intimidate, but to challenge. I crack my neck to the left, then to the right. I close my fists. I'm ready to party.

"Randy Jones," the one in front says. His demeanor and the fact that he stands a few feet ahead of the group makes me think he's the leader of this shit club. Also, his swastika tattoo is the only one with an open eye peeking from the center. It winks at me. "We've heard a lot about you."

"Well, I'm a popular guy. Got a pen? Paper? I'll be more than happy to give you girls my autograph."

Once one of the buildings for Medium security closed some of the more dangerous inmates got mixed with us in Minimum security. I don't know how the hell these guys could have come to this building. Maybe the others had overflowed; maybe things had gotten overlooked. Who the hell knows? But I had heard whispers from other cells at night; you don't want to be in the path of these maniacs. It's rumored they take their targets where they can't be seen, and then they perform rituals, sacrificing to some god they believe in.

"Yeah, we would love your autograph. How about signing the floor with your blood? You see, word around town is once you get out you plan on going to Death Highway."

Shit.

"Never heard of it." I lie. They know I'm lying. Wagers have been placed. I know for certain there's a bounty on my head. Maybe by some unhappy souls who are pissed about my last race. Trust me, I'm not too happy about it either.

The Nazi smiles, teeth crooked and the color of fly paper.

"Come on, Jones. No need to lie. Rumor has it, you aren't in it to race and play nice. You want to bring down the whole house."

I return his smile. Fuck it. We are already here, might as well play. "What can I say, I don't just want to bring it down. I want to set it ablaze and watch it all go up in smoke. Then piss on the ashes."

The eye glares at me from the Swastika. "You know there are a lot of people who've worked hard to get things the way they are and don't take kindly to your selfish little plan. Forfeit and join the Dead One. All will be forgotten; he rewards those who serve. You can race all you want; your family and friends will be safe. There's a place for everyone in the Red Plane."

It doesn't matter if I give in to their deal. I can see the blood lust in their eyes, the shanks gripped tightly in their hands. They plan on snuffing me out no matter what. So be it, I'm ready to fucking dance. My veins are pumping fire; I want to release a fury of hate on these bastards. Pain level shoots up to an eight. I don't remember the last time I took my pain killers, but it doesn't matter now. The pain heightens my senses. I close my right fist so tight the scars threaten to tear from my flesh.

"Last chance, Jones," he says. The others slowly close in. "Heed the call. Play by the rules or pay the debt."

I measure each one of them. They are all about my height, or slightly taller. All fit, very muscular, some slimmer than others. The one in the far back I'll have to keep an eye on; he's the biggest of the group, standing at least six feet and built like a brick house.

"Enough of the foreplay boys, you're going to do something, do what you got to do."

The smile on the leader's face broadens, stretches into insanity.

Before any of them get close, I'm already moving. My mind slows down time as I reach the work bench nearby. The leader advances on me. My hand grabs the wrench on the table and, in one quick motion, I strike him with it. As he stumbles backwards, hand to his bleeding mouth, I throw the wrench at the next Nazi coming in for the attack. There's a dense sound of metal striking skull as it bounces off his forehead. He falls backward and hits the floor, stunned momentarily.

If the leader wasn't choking on his teeth after taking a mouth full of wrench, he's going to now. I bring his head down to my knee, bones crack when I make contact. I move quickly, pulling him to the work bench.

I force his shank free and impale his hand on the wooden table.

Now he's screaming. I let him thrash wildly, like a fish on a hook, as I fight the next onslaught of Nazi hate. I fight off the shanks with blocks and counters, receiving cuts on my hands and forearms in the process. While I stun one with a shot to the throat, I manage to steal his weapon. I quickly stab one in the stomach, countering his attack. My motion goes from the stomach into his lower jaw; his mouth is a frozen scream. I see the blade of the shank between his teeth.

Pain rips into my right side. I back away, avoiding strikes while at the same time managing to take this Nazi's shank by breaking his arm. I stab him in the eye. Two down. I cry out in pain from an attack from behind. I reach behind me and pull the shank out of my left shoulder. The leader is back; the eye in the middle of his swastika is wide with madness. I move in to bring the blade across his throat. Blood seeps through his fingers as he pushes on his wound; he falls choking on his blood. Three down. The Nazi I've stunned with the wrench is on his feet joining one of his buddies to deliver another bolt of furious attacks. I manage to fight them off, ending one of their lives by stabbing him in the side of his head; he falls sideways, crashing down like a chopped tree. For the next one, I step aside, throw my arms up around his head and break his neck.

The next two come in strong; the blades of their shanks slice across my chest, my stomach. My hands move fast, my own weapons in each hand, my rage is a blur of red. They fall face down, blood pools around their bodies.

My muscle shirt, once white, is a deep crimson. I know I have some serious damage; I expected it. The pain kept my mind from the outside world's shuddering death throes.

One left. The big guy.

He was already moving, while I was finishing up with the last two of his buddies. The shank looks like a toy knife in his boulder size hands. He moves fast, faster than I have ever seen a man his size be able to do; my body buckles forward at the sheer force of his attack. His shank is sticking out of my stomach. He smiles at me, his mouth a checkerboard of missing teeth.

"We're going to get ours. Once you die, we reap The Dead One's rewards."

I stare at the shank, noticing the handle was nicely made. It's handled with a wood so dark red it's almost black. A tentacle is carved into it, twirling into the hilt, into my stomach. I admire its impressive handy work, even as the big goof pulls it out of me and stabs me again. Then again. The pain has me doubled over. I don't fall to my knees, fuck that. Instead, I smile, thick red spittle drools from my lips.

I have a little surprise for him.

I close my right fist.

I channel the pain and anger into that fist, the scarred flesh wiggles all along my arm, then tightens to the point my arm is taut, powerful. My arm is a hammer.

I punch my fist through the Nazi's stomach. I see my hand holding the clump of ropey intestines on the other side. I give a satisfying squeeze, crushing them between my fingers. I look in his terrified face. He's trying to speak, his mouth trying to work through the pain.

"How... how the fuck?"

"Give The Dead One my regards." I yank back my hand, pulling the string of his intestines with it, holding them up so that's the last thing he sees.

His large body falls back, hits the floor hard. The last of them is dead. It's over, but I'm still full of that surging red hot rage. I wish there were more to kill. I throw the Nazi's guts on his upturned face.

Dave, the rat son of bitch guard, hasn't turned around to check if the deed is done yet. I still have time. I am time and space.

I close my eyes. Blot out the pain in my dying body. Breath in, then out, just like the prison counselor taught me.

I open my eyes; my vision is wavy, a heat mirage dances in front of my eyes. I reach forward; my fingers

pierce the shaky air. I pull it apart like I'm swimming through a body of water. The tear fills with red and I step through.
I'm in the Red Plane.

The air is thick, my skin tingles. I fight to take off my muscle shirt; it sticks to my flesh with my blood. Every movement hurts. I throw it to the ground, let this alien world take it. I hiss through my teeth; my weakened body shakes to the point of convulsions. Stay focused, I tell myself; don't let the pain take you. The Red Plane will take care of the damage.

I survey the land around me. I have been here before. I don't remember how many times or why. The mountains around me are gigantic in size; they seem to reach forever into the blood red sky. Something screams above, the powerful sound of wings is rumbling through the sky as the thing passes overhead, the shadow engulfs everything around me for a moment before it moves on. I don't want to be here long, but I can't leave until the process is done.

I watch my body heal itself. The pain of my insides healing was the worst; once I got through that, the rest of the healing was manageable. The dying cells continue to regenerate, new tissue rebuilds itself, the wounds seal. The pink flesh itches; I refrain from scratching it. The soft flesh is now hardened. The healed wounds have the same look as the scars on the right side of my body.

I return to my world, the newly healed wounds are very tight; the lack of mobility is challenging, I am fatiguing quickly. But I still have a little more left in me to take on one more asshole.

The door squeaks open. The interloper steps in.

Dave the Correctional officer stops, and stares disbelieving at the bloody carnage. Then his eyes move to me.

"Oh shit."

He turns to run. I stretch my open palm in the direction of the door; I can feel its energy. I pull back and the door closes in Dave's face. He grapples with it, trying desperately to get it open, but that sucker is sealed shut.

I'm running out of the time. Soon the fatigue will overtake me and my body will be useless. I move as quickly as I'm allowed. I slam Dave against the door, place the shank up to his throat.

"Don't kill me, oh please don't fucking kill me!"

"Who waged this shit show?"

"I don't know! I never see their faces; they're always blurry, charred and featureless. Fucking things creep me out every time! Come on man, I'm just the messenger."

"Just a messenger, huh?"

"Yes, for fuck sakes! I was told there were Nazi Occultists in the prison. Once the Red Plane began its convergence, they began sacrificing people to the Dead

One. So, the wagers took advantage of their loyalty! Man, once those things found out your intention, they were pissed."

"What does the Dead One have on you?"

"Look," he says, his voice trembling; he's almost in tears. "I have a family, man. I'm sorry this happened to you, but I don't get paid enough, I. I needed more money! Ok! I know it's a fucking shitty excuse but what the hell am I supposed to do! You know these things, it's hard to say no. I hear the rewards are well worth it."

"No. They're not. Are there others?"

"That want to kill you? No. Only the skin heads were ordered to." Dave swallows hard, "You're safe, at least until you're released."

"You and any of your buddies involved going to clean this up? Keep this shit, hush hush?"

"That's the plan."

I lower the shank. I couldn't help myself so I gave him my award winning, shit eating grin. "Great. Here's what you can do for me. New uniform and a hot shower. I get a reward for surviving, right?"

Dave nodded rapidly.

I watch in awe as a conspiracy unfolds before my eyes. I knew this prison had done some shady shit, but this seemed even more astounding to me. Maybe it's because now we are adding interdimensional beings into the mix. I count five Correctional Officers, including Dave. They move quickly, piling the bodies onto hospital beds the other officers brought in. One of the Officers, a young kid who looked like he just started yesterday, was mopping up the blood. There was no way they could get through the prison without others noticing, unless they had a way out through the back. I wasn't sure. One thing was for certain, for this to occur, The Warden had to be involved, and many others as well. They may not want to get their hands dirty, but they'd have no problems averting their eyes.

"Wait a sec." I walk up to the two guards who have the leader's body on a bed.

The leader may be dead, but that eye, that damn eye in the middle of the swastika, is still moving, surveying its surroundings. Taunting me. I grab the shank next to the body and stab it and give the hilt a nice twist for good measure. The pupil explodes, the blood runs down the body adding to the madness of the tattoos. The two officers exchange disgusted looks, then wheel him away.

Once in the shower, I let the hot water pound my aching body. It washes away the blood, the pain, and the tightness in my body. I could fall asleep standing up. This is the most glorious thing I've ever experienced during my two year stay here, and I had to kill a bunch of scumbags to do it. I think of those old days, when I used to race for the thrill of it. Until money got involved. Then the Dead One. The old stir of temptation wells up inside of me. I am confident I could win many races again. I think of the outside world, almost there. I think of my home; I choke on despair. Fuck the call. I'm going to Death Highway.

    I'm going to get my life back.

2.

The prison is more menacing when I look at it from the outside. The many buildings that are part of its structure are deceased carcasses full of maggots. I can hear the prisoners inside; the sound of chaos erupts. The alarms go off. Gun shots ring out. In the prison yard, it's every man for himself as they rip into each other with their bare hands, but they are not hands at all; they are claws. The yard is soaked by the insides spilled from piles upon piles of bodies. The sky twitches, it's red. A blue lightning bolt strikes the sky like an exploding vein.

Nothing is familiar here. All the construction the state has done, building the Chapel Strip mall, adding restaurants, and stores and turning the old insane asylum into a condo, it's like nothing has happened. The buildings are hollowed out, reverting to their dark and cryptic pasts. Even though the buildings are a mile out, I can see the many eyes peering from the shadows of the place. The red plane has this place in its grip. The doorway is the history of this place; so much pain and death, the other world laps it up with its blistered tongue.

I turn away from it. When I do, a muscle car pulls up to the entrance of the prison. I know that car very well.

Laura's purple Barracuda. I do not smile. This is not real. Neither is the man walking to her car, his steps extra light on the day of his release. I see them embrace once he is in the car. Lies. Lies are the pulse of the Red Plane. I close my eyes. I remind myself I still have control. I feel the air shift. I open them. The Red Plane is gone, shoved back underneath the surface of the world I thought I knew. The prison is back to the normal brick buildings; the Insane Asylum is a condo again; the world is back to what I remembered before going to Prison. I can still sense its desolation. I won't take my hand and peel away the surface. This place is still trying desperately to hold me in its grasp.

Not expecting anyone to pick me up, I make my way to Pontiac Boulevard. It's going to be a long walk home. That's ok, I know there is nothing waiting for me, but, in order for me to start this journey, I need to get started.

Pontiac Boulevard was normally a very busy main road. At certain times of the day, cars would be jam packed, bumper to bumper, waiting for the slow death of the light, and then the light after. Just when you thought you were out of the traffic, you would reach the elementary school up ahead.

I am walking down Pontiac Blvd during a work day, and even then, it was always jammed with cars. Hardly a single vehicle passes by me. Twenty minutes into my walk, I had seen one sporadically, either at the fast food restaurant to my left or coming out of the CVS lot to my right.

I stay away from the people sharing the sidewalk with me. They are shambling things. Like the lack of cars driving around, the people are sporadic as well. When one does appear, I circle around them, keeping a wide berth. One person that passed I wouldn't even consider human anymore. I could smell the death wafting off him, even when I took a chance and walked in the deserted street. He's not wearing the dirty clothes of a normal bum; this guy is a business man. Surprisingly, his suit looks almost brand new, but so do the things blistering all over his face. I turn away when things begin to squirm within the yellow colored baseballs on his face. I dare not turn around when I hear something pop, something landing on the sidewalk with a wet sound.

Even though I have some knowledge of the thing I've become, and knowledge of the Red Plane, I did not realize my world had changed so quickly. Was what I was witnessing outside the prison a glimpse or, as I suspected, just under the surface like the things on that man's face. I'm afraid I have no choice but to witness reality bursting and unleashing ungodly things all over this town.

Another shambling creature. His white tee shirt is dirty and torn, his left side leans. I can hear his neck creek as he turns to look at me as I walk by.

"Interloper," he hisses.

I stop in my tracks. I turn my head toward the vile thing.

"What did you say?"

I shouldn't waste time talking to this thing. But part of me, the part that feeds on high octane racing and bloodied fists fights, can't turn away from an adversary. This place has made me antsy; my right side is itching to punch through another body.

It barely pays any more attention to me as it answers with another long hiss, and then continues its way in the other direction.

My feet move quicker, even as they grow tired and my legs ache. It feels like it'll take forever to get to my house, but, then again, I don't think time is normal anymore as the axis tips. The cold breeze feels nice like autumn, but everywhere I look there's a shimmer, like a heat mirage on the hottest summer day. There are other things in the shadows; they lurk behind the far away abandoned buildings, and closer behind the decrepit homes.

I am sad, but not surprised to find, as I draw closer to my own neighborhood, the houses there don't look any better. I fought the urge to look in these homes, these pallid faces glaring at me so malevolently. The paint, peeled away long ago, reminded me of shredded skin revealing the rawness beneath. The windows are boarded up with two by fours that go across each other in the shape of an X, dead eyes. I don't care for the stares; I don't need to know the secrets the faces want to share with me.

I have my own to deal with.

So, I keep walking; it's hard to bear witness to what I've felt settle inside me during the time I've spent in prison. Now I am questioning if that was real at all.

My house sways back and forth. I can't move my feet. All the Nazi Occultists in the world cannot instill the sweltering fear I am enduring when I see my own home, once a sanctuary Laura and I worked so hard to build, is now a living, breathing organism of this nightmarish world. I see the Red Plane laughing in the pale sky over head.

I'm having an out of body experience when I finally start walking toward the front steps. My mind is collapsing. Laura is with me, holding my hand, smiling, her green eyes standing out against the opaqueness of crimson slowly shadowing above. She's pulling me up the front steps, too fast. I want to tell her to slow down, stop, just give me a minute.

The old wooden steps groan underneath each step; I nearly cry out when she opens the door. The hinges screech at me like a banshee.

I stand in the doorway. Alone. Laura is gone, was never here in the first place, not on this plane at least. My mind is colliding with the images drilled into it, images I dare not wish for. I will not fall for bullshit trickery. I know the Red Plane wants me to focus on those lost desires, wants me to choose between there and here. What person, in their right mind, wouldn't choose to be with the person they love, smiling and laughing?

Somewhere, deep in the catacombs of my home, a baby cries.

I almost go to it, thinking someone has left their child in my house. I take a deep breath. Why am I doing this to myself? To test myself, that is why. Besides shoving opioids down my throat to fight pain, and antidepressants to fight my anxiety, my mind was clear when I was in prison. The ceiling was blank. My head is heavy, while traveling the outside world, muddy with the possibilities of other lives. Reluctantly, I step over the threshold, right foot first, then follows the left. I prepare myself before jumping into the sea of memories; I don't want to drown in their undertow. I am in the living room; the furniture floats in the imaginary waves like bloated corpses. I run my hand along the cushions, recoiling in disgust at its damp moldiness. Immediately upon touching the ruined furniture, a smell like a dead, wet dog overwhelms my senses, causing my eyes to water.

It's funny how the sight of these materialistic items instills an exhausting sadness within me. Within that slither of a moment, I don't want to move on. The house shudders, voices crawl within the walls of my old home. I hear Laura and, suddenly, I am holding her in my arms. She's looking up into my face with those emerald green eyes I love so much; her smile is beaming like the sun soaking in through the windows.

"So? What do you think?"

I'm so lost in her I have no idea what she's talking about. "Huh?"

"The couches, silly!"

I turn around. A large couch, material a charcoal grey, is up against the wall. On the other side, closest to the front, is a smaller couch, with matching color and material.

"They're nice," I say to her.

"Nice?" she asks, her voice heavenly. I feel like I haven't heard it in years. I haven't. "That's all you got to say?"

"Well, I mean I did live with my Grandparents most of my life, and they had the same furniture since I was a kid."

She laughs at that. I find myself laughing with her.

She plants a kiss on my lips, and then pulls herself out of my arms. I'm standing there with my arms still open. I feel like a part of me has been torn away. I almost pull her back so I can stay in this memory just a little while longer.

"Come on! Let's get this plastic off and enjoy our new couches!"

I turn around. The couches are not new anymore; they are in the moldy ruin of decay and despair I had found them in. The sun is gone; the coldness inside is just as ominous as the living grayness outside. The sky flashes, grey turns red, then back to grey.

I need to move on. I don't have much time. The Red Plane is devouring my home and everything around it very slowly. The dying feeling is stronger now, settling in like rigor mortis. The Red Plane will use every form of trickery to keep me here. Before I cross the threshold into the dining room, I hear something stir behind me. When I turn around, I see a young man lying on the soggy couch; it squelches under his movement. The right side of his face is badly scarred just like mine. It's almost a mirror image but then I realize I am staring at a younger me; another memory makes itself known. I don't like the look on his face; it's full of such disdain I'm afraid it's as infectious as the merging of the worlds. His left arm hangs off the couch, in his hand an open bottle of whiskey. He takes a big pull from it, his eyes never leaving me. When he's done drinking the bottle, he holds it up. I can smell it from here, my mouth waters.

"Want some?"

"I'm good." I turn from him, wanting to continue forward. I had left this version of me behind years ago.

"You think you're so much better than me, don't you?"

I don't turn back to him when I simply answer, "Yes."

Once I was cleared to come home, after spending months healing in the hospital, I had immediately descended into a tunnel of anger and self-pity. that I spent more time drinking on the couch than going to physical therapy and having more skin graft surgeries. I took the pain killers at least; they went down easily with the whiskey. It was a burn I relished, more than the ones I had to live with.

Laura had had enough; she had left the house crying and had gone to my grandfather for help. He had come by that day and given me a good heart to heart talk. Not one full of kittens and rainbows either. The entire time he laid into me about how I was lucky to have a girl like Laura to take care of me when it was my fault all of this had happened. I could see his fingers knotted in each other. He had desperately fought taking his giant hands and wrapping them around my throat. I would've deserved it, trust me.

So yeah, I am better than that piece of shit glaring at me from his decayed couch. I ignore anything else he spits, and finally move into the dining room. Doing so, I assume he's gone, vanished back into the catacombs of a distant time. I hear the baby again; its cries echo from upstairs. I look warily at those stairs. There's nothing up there for me. I can see the small hallway in my head; the bathroom is the first door on the right, and then our bedroom. The room across from ours was supposed to be the nursery. Laura comes into my mind again. Our times spent in that bedroom, her pale skin on top of me, her fiery red hair in my face as we made love,; I can smell her sweet perfume, almost taste the sweat on her skin.

Where are you, Laura?

The walls are moving, forming shapes as they push outward. The yellow wall is a hand, outstretched and reaching for me. I almost dare to reach out, allow my finger tips to touch the fingers of the thing. It whispers to me, but I don't understand it's frantic babbling. I move away from it and make my way to the kitchen.

Thankfully, there aren't any illusions taunting me. The only thing I keep my eyes on a little bit longer is the patio table we had used as a kitchen table. It had belonged to Laura,; she's had it since her old apartment, bought it off a friend. It's one of those square tables with a glass center, an entry for the umbrella pole to go into. It added a nice little bit of charm to the kitchen, and besides it had saved us some money, so we hadn't had to buy a new one right away.

I walk over to the basement door; its pushing from its frame, rhythmically, like a heartbeat. It stops once I touch the door handle. My hand feels the energy in the door handle. This is where I need to go, the basement. I will get my answers there; I don't know why. I just do. I just have that feeling.

I turn the knob and pull open the door to darkness, the spiral of old rotted stairs comes out of the blackness once my eyes adjust. I flick the switch. Of course, it doesn't work. I don't think anything has worked in this house for a while, however long a while was here.

Taking my time, I go down the steps one by one, careful not to trip over the last couple of steps as darkness takes me. I stand there for a few moments, so my eyes can adjust. I see the outline of the washer and dryer in the back; the little bit of grey light sneaking through the dirty basement windows shows the touch of rust on the machines. I walk in that area, only to take a right into a smaller room.

All four walls are brick. Across from me, stacked upon each other, are numerous totes filled with stuff we couldn't fit into our home, and other totes full of holiday decorations. Ahead of me is where I want to go. The brick wall shimmers, the same mirage I had seen at the prison. This time when I reach into it, the fabric of reality does not tear. Instead, it falls open, brick by brick. My fingers rake against the wall and more bricks fall, revealing an open space. I continue to pull more bricks from the foundation. The shimmering is still there, but much stronger. It makes my vison seem blurrier. I pull it open; the tear fills with red. I step in, foot first, without even thinking about what could be on the other end. When I entered the Red Plane from the Prison, I was able to see where I would end up, and, even then, I didn't want to stay long because of the huge things that own the sky.

  I have a strong urge to follow my gut. I just go through; I somehow know I will be fine. It's better than dealing with my memories haunting me on the floor above. Something is telling me I'll get answers here. Once I am through the fissure, I am in a cave. The rock is the color of molten lava. I smell sulfur but it's not cloying; it just exists. I see a duffel bag up ahead and go over to it; it is familiar to me. I remember hiding this, some time ago, in another life.

  In that life, it was right before the accident. Things had been heating up, even though we rid ourselves of our enemies, the other racing gangs, by joining the Dead One's world. It had been Chris's idea, someone who was our bookie and I had thought was a friend, at the time. He said the crew and I would be wheelmen for him, doing small jobs, mainly picking up items that were owed, money, guns, etc. This is where Laura wanted out, and, while she understood why I needed to stay a little longer, she didn't judge me, until the bullets flew way more than often, and the battle had hit home.

I unzipped the bag. Just as I had expected, guns. Lots of them. I had stolen them from another racing gang's safe house. I remember the bullets flying because I was the one that had shot first. They had the balls to send one of their guys to my house, with Laura home. At that point, we were engaged and had just found out she was pregnant.

They fired on the house. Laura was hurt. I went after them.

"Randy Jones."

The voice is powerful, the entire interior of the massive cave shook from whomever was able to project it. I look up from the bag and gasp. To my amazement, the wall in front of me has formed a shape; the thing is a writhing mass of appendages and insectile legs and claws. Its body seems to stretch out amongst most of the wall in this area of the cave.

"What are you?"

"I am The Eye of Beholder of The Red Plane."

3.

I am in awe of this god like creature spread out before and all around me. It's one eye is the size of an automobile. I am staring at multiple rows of teeth because it has multiple mouths. When it spoke, all the mouths spoke at once, sounding like a loud and powerful echo. The tentacles have pulled from the rock, and now its black and red flesh surrounds me, but not in a threatening way. I see it as being curious, as in an eye of the beholder kind of way.

"I thought the eye of the beholder was supposed to represent some kind of beauty?" I know it's not the best of ideas to start out being a smart ass, but I have never really stopped before, so why should I start now. Giant tentacle cave god be damned.

"There's beauty in the chaos of the universe, is there not," the many mouths answer.

"Ok. Good point," I say, "What the fuck are you doing in my basement, or part of it?"

"You asked for me."

I scoff. "Not by name."

"You're looking for answers, are you not?" it responds.

Now it's got me. "Yes. That is true. And you'll have them for me? No offense, Mr. Beholder, but there are things out there that want me dead and my own home tried attacking me with my memories. So, a creature with many mouths and tentacles claiming to hold beauty that has answers to my questions leads me to be a little skeptical."

The mouths laugh. I guess you could call it a deep belly laugh; the ground shook beneath my feet.

"I could consume you within seconds and your soul would be lost within the abyss." The mouths threaten all at once.

"Then why don't you?"

"Because you are the merger of all things. You have to go to Death Highway."

"Yes, I do."

"But not just for the reasons you seek."

I couldn't find the words I wanted to speak. I mean, why wouldn't I go to Death Highway for what I seek, isn't that the point?

"Selfishness will not truly close all the doors and keep them locked. You can never truly destroy or stop the Red Plane from existing, but you can lock away a version of it. The most threating one of them all."

"The one we are all in," I say.

"Yessss," the many mouths hiss.

"Why are you helping? Aren't you a part of this world?"

"I am. But I do not wish for our world to consume another. I do not share the jealousy of many of this plane. The moment The Wayfarer introduced waging bets, the door was opened, and many have lost their way."

"Wayfarer? You mean the Dead One."

"Eyeless." The many mouths hiss again.

"Stop that; that's creepy."

"Reach into the bag," it says, ignoring my comment.

I do as it asks. My hand shuffles through the numerous guns, small and large, also boxes of ammo for those guns. My hand wraps around something that does not feel like a handgun or an automatic rifle. It's thick in diameter and has a chiseled shape to it. I pull out the statue and hold it up.

"I have seen this before," I say.

"It is the true form of the Dead One. It's used as a challenge to his human form. You can bend the rules of Death Highway with such a powerful thing, but you can't do this alone."

"That I know. I am looking for my friends. I am looking for Laura."

"Keep that statue with you; it's power will help the one you have insight. You can't just open fissures into the Red Plane, you also can hop to different realities."

"Really? That's cool."

"The statue will help you pinpoint your destination, and that way you won't get lost."

I observe the ugly thing before placing it back into the bag. It's got a tusk for a head; the pointed end reaches to the middle of its back, where there are wings not spread, but folded. It perches on a mound of skulls. But's that is all I could truly make out of this creature that is supposed the Dead One, which I only seen in his human form, this thing is much more frightening than the mass before me.

"So where do I start?"

"Once you find your entrance, it will take you where you need to go. There are others who have been in your presence when you were burning in between worlds."

I swallow hard; memories of being on my hospital bed, delirious from the pain, then completely wacked out from the morphine push into my head. While I fought through that and the intense shivering, I kept blanking out. Each time I would see a different face. Laura's. My Grandparent's. The faces of my crew, minus Cody. As time passed, I could've sworn there was something strange about those days in the hospital. While I was in prison, I chalked it up to possibly The Red Plane slowly converging around that time, or that I was just too hopped up on pain and drugs to fully grasp what was going on.

"First," the beholder continues, "you must seek out the Place of Chariots. After that is located, your ability will strengthen. It will be easier to locate the rest of your chosen ones. You will have to go to the land of the Contaminated. That part of your world has almost completely merged with the Red Plane, where your home is will shortly follow."

"Lovely," I say, "Then what?"

"Then the Testimony of Truth. After your circle is complete, you will be able to face the deceiver. Until then, I strongly advise not doing so until your group is assembled. There is one you have to watch out for though; he is the worst."

"Who is that?"

"Alter Inhorruit."

"What the hell? Come on Beholder, you been speaking English just fine, and you throw that at me. What is that, Latin?"

"Yes. It's what he calls himself."

"Ok. And it means what?"

"The Scarred One."

I sigh. That doesn't sound good.

"Once you reach Death Highway, you will all find your fates. Now go, Randy Jones. I grow weak and your worlds above are colliding. You need to get to the first passageway before it takes you within its grasps. You have enemies waiting, so be careful."

"Thank you. I hope I can make things right."

"As do I."

The Beholder melds back into the rocky cavern it had grown from. The spot where the mass was is now just black and red fissures across rock. I turn to find the fissure hasn't closed. I walk through, my feet find purchase on my basement floor, back in the small room. I hurry upstairs. Once in the kitchen, I find the house is shuddering. The walls are breaking apart, arms reach out, bloodied. I see the faces of many people from my life, all looking to get a hold of me. I see other versions of me, ready to collide and collapse and change into what this place breeds. I take the .38 I took out of the bag from my jeans and fire a couple of shots at the other versions of me; they drop with bullets in their heads. Their heads break open; something insect-like, hissing madly, climbs out from the tops of the heads. I stomp on the disgusting things. Another version of me is all scars; he smiles like a madman. I leave out the side door, hurry down the steps, and run across the yard to stand on the driveway.

Many eyes stare at me from inside of my home. It's not my home anymore. It belongs to the many versions of me, and the different variations of my memory. It's their home now, a haunted fucking house. They can have it. Watchful eyes not only peer at me from my home, but from the houses around me. Across the street, a pale thing with long stringy hair stands in its doorway; it looks like it's deciding if it is going to run out the door at me. In the yard one over, a small boy watches me from underneath the porch. He's hunched over, most of the hair on his head is gone, the scalp revealed by patches of fallen hair. He hisses at me and then comes out of his hiding spot, black talons scurrying up the steps before disappearing into the house through the side door.

The sky is exploding. Like the beholder has said, this reality is merging with the Red Plane . Place of Chariots. I have to think quickly, and then it clicks. Of course, that's where I must go next; it makes sense. I investigate the black maw of my garage. My car is not there; the emptiness is swirling, a churning tunnel of black mass.

"Don't do it, Randy."

I know that voice. I turn around and see Chris standing in my driveway. He wasn't there before, and now, suddenly, appears out of nowhere. Just from the wasted look of him, I can tell he's not here for a friendly chat and catch up. Not that I would want that with this son of a bitch.

"Chris." I say to the nightmarish thing that was once a human being, once a friend. "What are you doing here?"

"Stopping you from making a big mistake," he says, taking a few steps forward.

I raise the revolver and point it at him. He stops, raises his hands, a big smile on his face.

Seeing him closer is even more disturbing.

The man I used to know, the one who used to book our races, pick the spots, make sure they were good paying races and the spots weren't widely popular with the police, the man who promised us we could take over the city of Providence in underground racing, make street racing big in Rhode Island. But then he had gotten involved with the wrong people, started owing those groups money, which, in turn, brought the heat onto us. The only way he could settle that debt was to give his soul to the Dead One. Unfortunately, he pretty much forged all our names and sold ours as well.

"I don't think you're going to stop anything, not with the way you look."

He brings his hand to his cheek and looks at the blood. "Oh, that. That's nothing. Just a little price I must pay to make full ascension, as you can see." He raises his hands to the sky, always the showman, always had to exaggerate everything. "As you can see, it is about to happen; well, on this plane at least. I see you found a wormhole."

"Yeah, and I'm going through it and ending this shit storm you started."

He shakes his head back and forth slowly. "I didn't start this, Randy. You're the catalyst. You're the one who opened the door; I just helped find the key."

"Fuck you." I should pull the trigger, but I don't think he's worth the bullet. I see shapes moving in closer, slowly surrounding me. How much more damage could Chris do in his state? He looks like he is slowly decomposing right before my eyes.

The wind is starting to pick up. In my backyard, a tree crashes down. Another one, much smaller, tumbles over weakly in the front; its trunk bends like rubber. The reality of this plane is turning elastic. The sky slowly starts to bleed.

"Isn't this beautiful!" Chris yells.

Screw this, I'm shooting him. But, as I am about to pull the trigger, I swing my right hand in the direction of movement in the corner of my eye and quickly fire. The head of the creature that was about to attack explodes. Its dark and scaly body falls limply to the ground. There's the sound of talons scurrying on my garage roof; I aim above me just as another creature leaps from the roof. It takes a bullet in the mouth; half its jaw is missing. It lands next to me; I stomp on it a few times until it doesn't move. Two more creatures make their way toward me; they are so fast that, if I even dared to turn around and jump into the swirling darkness, they would succeed in injuring me. They go down, head shots as well. Then I aim at Chris and pull the trigger.

Click. The chamber's empty.

He bellows out laughter. "You lost count, you stupid fuck!"

I take my chances and make a run into my garage. The black swallows me; I am running through a swirling tunnel instead of an actual garage. The other end opens slowly, showing another realm to enter. Before I enter, I hear Chris's voice echo in the chamber.

"I'll see you soon!"

I step out into another plane; the wormhole disappears behind me.

4.

There's an opening on the end, a small circular opening. It expands as I move closer, revealing an entirely different neighborhood. Thankfully, it was not the opaque breathing red I had escaped moments ago.

I step through the opening. The wormhole starts to dissipate behind me as it continues its circular rotation, getting smaller until it winks out of existence.

Having to scan the area, it takes me a few minutes to fully recognize where I am. The wormhole dropped me right where I needed to be, imagined to be. It's an amazing power to have, but I won't lie and say that it doesn't fill me with trepidation. I can do all these things, but still don't have a full grasp of how or why. The only way I can explain any of this is once I get that feeling, that maddening itch deep inside my flesh, more so on the right side, I know what I need to do. So far, I have found I can punch through a human body, which, I'm not going to lie, was kind of fun. I have slight telekinesis and now I can open portals to what, another area of the same plane? A different plane?

What the fuck am I?

The one thing I do know is I am fucking exhausted. Every time I use this unknown power it drains me, causing a different type of pain, one brought on from fatigue and it hurts to move a part of the right side of my body.

On this long stretch of road, it's mostly an industrial area. Along the right side sit numerous shops and warehouses. On the left side, a street leads up to another neighborhood, and a large playground. If I were to walk in that direction and turn onto that street, it would lead me to my Grandparents' house. I am not in the mood for more talking walls and angry memories, but I can't help wanting to see a younger me playing at that playground, like the days when I'd visit my grandparents and they'd take me there to play. When I started living with them, that playground became a forgotten place, one only a child would go to. I was not a child anymore, despite my age.

I turn to the building across the street from me. I have another ghost to visit.

From the outside, Blackmore Autobody and Repair looks the same as it did years ago. A large warehouse building, with a slanted roof. The rectangular fence surrounding it reaches all the way to the back. On the top, the fence is decorated with barbed wire; although, from the state of things around here, I doubt this place is need of any type of security any more. The gate is open. I wonder if anyone has been here in quite some time.

The empty lot is depressing. When I used to work here, this place was flourishing with work. There were so many cars they filled the lot from the front to the back, and then there were the ones inside the shop that were being worked on. Even though I know they are not real, the sounds of grinding metal, sanding, and air compressor guns bring me comfort, bring me back to the good old days, when I had enjoyed the hard work and hadn't yet let street racing consume me.

At least the building isn't shuddering and shaking madly like my house was doing earlier, but the ghost still hurt. I open the door; it releases a sigh as it pushes inward. Or was that sigh coming from me? I walk through.

The office is the first part of the shop I enter. It's darker in here than outside, but I can make out the furniture just fine, with the grey light coming in from the outside. The furniture is not moldy with decay like the furniture in my house. It's just abandoned, and, for some reason, that bothers me even more. Just like the lot void of vehicles.

I am longing to see Karen Waterman behind that desk, looking at me as her small round glasses slip down her nose. A smile and then a big hug. And it would be a good hug, too. Not only was she the book keeper, and the person who handled the quotes on the type of work needed, she was kind of the den mother of all the boys at the shop. She kept them in line. She was a workout freak and was always trying to get everyone healthy. She always wore her workout clothes to work, that stretchy thermal type of material.

We would always talk about working out, Karen and me. Sometimes John would get in there, being the ball buster that he was. One time, we were sitting in the office during lunch and John chimed in while Karen and I were talking.

"Follow one of my routines, I bet neither one of you would come back, I'd work you so hard."

Karen gave him that look with the glasses, her eyes pointing at his belly.

"The only thing you're super setting right now is the beer bottles."

I laughed.

John Slater pats his belly with a smile. Then he says, "I wouldn't be like this if Randy and his grandfather weren't slackers; we used to work out in the basement all the time."

"Don't blame his grandfather," Karen scolded him, "And besides, most of the time, it's what you put in your mouth. Here have some salad." Karen held out her fork, some green leaves and a couple of strawberries attached to it.

He had waved it away with disgust. "Get the fuck out of here with that! Is that fruit in a salad? What kind of weird shit are you eating? What's that brown crap on it?"

"Balsamic Vinaigrette?"

John takes a bite out of his burger. "No thank you," He had said, as he was chewing at the same time.

Karen had shaken her head. "At least lose the fries."

I smile at that memory; it's less hurtful than the demons occupying my house. I must move forward though; I can feel the dying inside of me again. The Red Plane is gaining strength, moving into worlds like a tsunami.

I exit the office through a door and now I am inside the body shop itself. Surprisingly, the large open space isn't completely void of cars. A few vehicles are scattered about, but they look like they were being worked on at one point and then all activity just ceased. Like whoever was working on them had left in a hurry.

I wonder what it would be like if everything was normal. I picture myself as just an ex street racer having done time for breaking the law. I still have my scars from the accident, and, even though I have had my challenges in the past, the programs had helped me. I do everything right before I finally come home. Would Laura greet me with a smile? Would Karen give me one of her strong hugs? At the car to my right, I could imagine John sanding it, his huge forearms tight as he moved the sander in circular motions along the surface of the car door. Would he greet me with one of his strong handshakes and make one of his jokes?

"Hey kid! How's the outside world treating ya? You coming back to work or staying home on the couch watching shows all day?"

I don't know how it would've played out if The Red Plane hadn't happened. I move through the open space, dreamlike, head heavy again. I rip my mind from the memories, from what could've happened, and stay focused on what should happen. I make my way to the back of the shop; the garage door at the back is open. I see her sitting there, waiting for me.

My Midnight Beauty. But the 1972 Oldsmobile is not alone, other familiar muscle cars line up along the fence with her. The chariots. War beasts. Next to Midnight Beauty, Jack's 1969 Dodge Charger. Then Alex's 1970 Chevy Chevelle. Will's Pontiac GTO, and finally, Laura's 1970 Plymouth Barracuda. All here, all ready to race together. I walk over to her and run my hand along the dark blue surface. Oh how I have missed her. The dark blue reminds me of the deepest parts of the ocean, but, at night, she's a shadow in the dark, moving so fast the eye won't catch her, unless it's under the moon's brightest of light, or the illumination of street lights overhead.

"You deserve this, Randy."

I spin around. I am no longer in the back lot of Blackmore Autobody. I am back home with my Grandparents.

"You've worked hard," Grandpa says. He and Grandma are standing by the garage. He has his arm around grandma, and they are smiling. This is a proud moment for them, as it is for me.

"You kept your word, got your school grades high, stayed out of fights, so we kept our word."

I remember the feeling of this day, the nervous excitement when I got home from school. The bus had dropped me off. I saw the large shape in the driveway immediately. Even though it was covered under a tarp, I knew a car when I saw one. I found it strange he had covered it. Maybe it was another car Grandpa planned to work on once he was finished with the previous one? Grandpa saw me immediately when the bus dropped me off. By the time I had walked up the driveway, he had excitedly called Grandma to come outside, and then I had known this was not a side job he was doing; this was for me.

I pulled off the tarp to reveal the 1972 Oldsmobile, just like the one he used to have. I had fallen in love with that car when I was young and was sad when he had sold it to help a friend, even though he had chalked it up getting too old for fast cars.

The car hadn't been painted yet. Most of the original paint had been stripped so the car's surface had been reduced to its original look, grayish chrome with some spots of its old paint still on in places. It had needed some sanding done and other work before it could be painted. That was not my area of work; I already knew where would send it to have it done.

"I'll pay for the paint job when you graduate high school," Grandpa said. "It's drivable but will need work. I figure me and you can work on it together on the weekends, as long as you continue with your school work."

"You got it," I said, not able to hide the wide smile on my face. I walked over to them and wrapped my arms around my grandparents. My right arm just barely wrapped around Grandpa's broad frame, while my left arm easily scooped up Grandma in my awkward, yet affectionate embrace.

The memory fades. I am back in the lot of the body shop.

"450 horse power. That baby right there is a 9 second car, just the way you left it."

I almost pull my gun on the person speaking to me. Jack Slater is already ahead of me, pointing a .45 handgun. I slowly raise my hands.

"Hey, Jack," I say.

"Randy, it's been a while. I knew I would find you here sooner or later."

"Memory is a little shaky but I seem to remember I gave Grandpa the rights to get my car out of the impound and get it here."

"Yeah," he says, still holding the gun. His hand is steady, he's got my head in his sights. "Dad and I decided to keep it here until you were out, and ready to pick it up. Figured it would be safer."

"That's good," I say. "You going to lower that now?"

"Is it really you, Randy?"

"Who else has this ugly mug?"

Jack laughs. It dies down quickly; his eyes look beyond me. "Friends of yours?"

I slowly turn my head, keeping my hands up, and survey the long stretch of grassless land beyond the fence. Standing on the train tracks are numerous figures, their flesh the color of soot. I must squint to fully focus on them; they are covered by the illusionary heat shimmer of the Red Plane. Soon, they'll cross over and take over this plane.

I turn back to Jack. "No, but I think we need to get the others soon and come back for our cars."

"Yeah, well, we are sticking to what you told us in the hospital."

"What I told you?"

He nods his head slowly. I relax when he finally conceals the handgun in the back of his jeans.

"I figure I'll fill you in on our way to get Alex. I don't think he's doing well."

I give Jack a questionable look. How does he know what's going on? It seems like he understands the mechanics of this world. I wonder if it's because that's how the merge affects people. Some go insane and change into horrid things, while others grasp a full understanding of the Red Plane's madness. The only one I have seen so far that understands it is Jack, and, if what he says is true about the things I said while in the hospital, I wonder if that's when it slowly began its merge and whoever was in the room with me was saved from the infection early on.

When he walks over to me, I embrace him with a big hug. I am extremely happy to see him, his is a familiar face amongst the insanity, and one that isn't out to get me. His looks have changed a little bit; he still wears his leather jacket, and engineer boots, but he has grown a beard. A couple years ago it was just a small beard that traced along his jaw line and into a small goatee, but this beard is a longer than that. I grab a fist full of it and give it a tug.

"Ow," he says, "What are you twelve?"

"I wanted to see if you are real," I laugh. "You didn't have that last time I saw you."

"Well, spending a lot of days in New Hampshire will do that to you."

"Oh really, yeah I can't wait to hear this," I say.

"What's in the bag?" he asks, nodding to the big duffel bag at my feet.

I unzip it, and then pull the bag open to reveal its contents. Jack whistles.

"We really are doing this, huh?" he asks.

"Yeah." I open the trunk and stick the bag in, then close it. My hands start to feel clammy. I don't know why but I am starting the onset of an anxiety attack. I fight against it and open the driver side door. The keys are already in the ignition. I sit in the leather bucket seats.

I should be excited. Jack and his dad have repaired my car to almost the exact way I had it before the accident. But instead of inhaling the new car smell, and enjoying this moment of reuniting with Midnight Beauty, I break into an intense sweat. I nearly hyperventilate, and still I continue to fight against it. I place my hands on the steering wheel.

I see fire. I smell burning flesh as it melds to leather. The sound of twisting metal fills my ears, and the panicked cries for help. My arms catch fire. There's a face peering up at me from the flames; the flesh falls off as his mouth opens in an eternal scream before the explosion rocks my brain. I jump out of the car screaming.

I keel over, hands on my knees and take deep breaths. I finally calm down and look over at Jack. His face is solemn; there's something in his eyes that says he half expected my reaction.

"Yeah, I had a feeling that was going to happen. I mean, shit dude, when was the last time you were in the car since the accident? Never, right?"

"I don't have time for this," I say, frustration in my voice.

Jack gets in the driver seat and turns the key. Midnight Beauty roars to life. Despite the attack, her idling purr relaxes me.

"Come on," Jack says, "I'll drive us to Alex's apartment. Hopefully, it'll help."

When I get in the passenger seat, it's not as bad. The anxiety is there only because I am in the car, but I'm not driving. How the hell am I going to go to Death Highway when I can't even drive my car without seeing images of the accident, like I am reliving the whole thing again? Hopefully, jumping realities will help dissipate that part of me.

Jack pulls the muscle car out of the back lot and to the front. He turns left onto the street, once he drives through the open fence. I can't help but think about the visions, something was different. When I was reaching for Cody to save him in my head, he wasn't reaching out to be saved, he was reaching out to pull me in.

5.

Jack wastes no time once we pull out of the body shop. He brings the car onto Roger Williams Boulevard, but he doesn't drive off yet. Midnight Beauty idles, I find her predatory purr relaxing me even more. He steps on the accelerator and revs the engine. She roars to life. He revs it a couple more times.

He looks over at me and smiles. I know that malicious smile, "I got something that'll cure your anxiety." He steps on the peddle again, relishing the sound as he's revving the engine. I find myself relishing it all over again, as well.

He's working the shifter and the clutch, and, within seconds, we reach fast speeds. I sink into my seat as Midnight Beauty charges forward, the screeching tires echo throughout the abandoned street. It's almost a territorial sound.

We are quickly approaching the stop sign. He looks over at me and smiles. "You know, I had a dream I died at that intersection, driving too fast?"

I raise my eyebrow. "Really?"

He smiles at me before he accelerates the car.

Once the front of Midnight Beauty crosses the intersection, the car lifts off the ground and sails through the air before landing. The suspension bounces around a bit, but nothing that would cause any damage. Jack continues at high speeds until we reach an overpass up ahead. He slows down to the normal speed limit.

"Hell yeah!" he screams, "That felt good."

It did. Any anxiety I had been feeling seems to slowly get left behind in the dust. Especially after that little stunt; my adrenaline is pumping. I haven't felt this alive in a long time. It feels has if the blurriness of this world is fading, leaving me clear headed. Then I start to think about Alex, worried about the state he might be in.

"His addiction is killing him," Jack says

"You know about that, too?" I ask, this new world is strange and full of surprises.

"I see a lot of weird shit, Randy." Something in his voice has changed. The thrill seeker now gone, his voice sounds haunted. "Ever since that day we were all in the hospital visiting you, we've all started experiencing weird shit. Then one day you grab a hold of me, the pain had gotten to you bad, and you said something like, 'It's coming. The Red Plane is coming; you need to prepare.'"

"And we did," Jack continues, "And since then, over the past couple years, the crew has begun to slowly split from each other. I think that is happening because of the convergence of the place you told us about. I keep seeing you, and you kept telling me more things about it."

"Shit. I don't remember any of this. Maybe bits and pieces, but only in dreams."

"Well, I mean you were supposed to be in a coma, Randy. But you got out of it and you were somewhere else. But because of what happened, Alex immediately turned to drugs, and Will is somewhere in the woods. He started playing commando after his paranoia got worse. You know how he is, being a conspiracy freak and all."

"Then," Jack continues, "After all of this, I began seeing my deaths. The other versions of me dying, either from a race gone bad, like you, or just some freak accident. I've seen my father die, many times."

"What? I'm sorry you have to experience that," I say.

"It happens a lot. I can't tell if it's a warning, or if it's other version of him dying the same way just to torment me. Then there're the things I've seen, what people are turning into." He grows silent, but only for a short amount of time, "We didn't even bother selling the shop. Nobody came. You see the roads; there's never anyone driving anymore. They walk around, confused and angry. So, we moved to our cabin in New Hampshire, until I had a dream you were out. I got dressed, said bye to dad and walked into the woods. Found you at the shop."

"You jumped realties?"

"Yeah, there was some tunnel, just there, swirling between trees, craziest shit I ever seen. I trusted it because, well since that day you grabbed my arm, I just started knowing things. I think all of us know a little something about what is happening since then."

This is exhausting. Even with my own understanding, I still don't know how it is I became what I am. Was it the statue? Was the Red Plane slowly making its merge when I got into the accident? What about the city of Providence and our little town Blackmore, what makes both places a target for the other dimension?

We grow silent. I am not a fan of silence; I fight the urge to turn on the radio or listen to a disc in the CD player. Some heavy metal would be great right about now.

Jack pulls up to the building Alex's apartment is located in. His eyes are wide when he sees the building is doing strange things, things a building shouldn't be doing. I've already seen this with my own home, but the house was alive with my own memories, good and bad. This building is a breeding ground of bad things. The building isn't breathing, or swaying back and forth, it's squirming. Parts of the building are moving around like there are things crawling all over it.

"We have to go in there?" Jack asks, his face has gone white.

"Yep." I don't want to wait any longer. I get out of the car. I check the cylinder of my snub nose; its full of all six bullets. Reloads are in the pocket of my leather jacket.

Jack double checks the clip of his hand gun. He nods to me; he's good to go.

We take our time climbing the stairs that line the outside of the apartments. On each floor, the walls are squirming with whatever has infected the building and its occupants. I make sure not to touch or go anywhere near any of the moving shapes. They are not aware of us, so it seems, but still we make sure not to run. Alex's apartment is on the third floor; we continue down the walkway, guns drawn. On the right, there are patio tables and a set of chairs for each one. On the left, we pass the apartments, four doors down we reach Alex's.

I reach for the door handle and look to Jack, who has grown two more shades of white; the fear is transparent. I don't blame him, I'm afraid as well. There is something sinister about this building and the things in it that give me a more insidious feeling than anything I've encountered so far. Jack nods for me to go ahead. I turn the handle, it's unlocked. I freeze as the door creaks open. I nearly scream when I see what's inside, what has become of Alex's apartment.

There's spider webbing everywhere, large amounts covering the walls, making the furniture non-existent. The things crawling all over the building, their shapes are more present in this room, less like the illusions we have seen all over the building. One scurries over the ceiling and goes into a different room in the apartment.

"Let's go," I whisper.

Jack groans, but follows anyway, staying close behind.

The apartment has a strange smell to it, the putrid scent is nearly intoxicating. On the far side of the apartment and to our right, there is a cocooned shape. I can tell by the legs and arms that it is a human being. I scan for the face.

"It's Alex."

"Are you sure?" Jack whispers, his eyes move around wildly, searching the ceiling for any of the creatures responsible for the webbing.

"Yes." I hiss. I touch the webbing that is holding him up against the wall. It feels strange as I rub it between my fingers. The sliver strings start to disintegrate, melting into a brownish color. The smell from earlier is now stronger, like something burning in tinfoil; my head feels light.

I remember how I was affected by the Red Plane and what Jack told me about Alex and his growing addiction.

"Don't touch the web." I hiss, trying my best not to raise my voice any louder, alerting the creatures in here. "It's made of heroin."

"What?"

Something drops to the ground behind Alex. We both jump at the thing that has come from its hiding spot on the ceiling. It's has a face similar to the blood hound creatures and a round head. No eyes, its head splits open into a mouth. Its attached to a chest that has multiple tiny arms; the chest and stomach lead into the round rear end of a spider, where the arachnid legs are located, four on each side. Before I can tell him to stop, Jack pulls out his hand gun and unloads four or five bullets into that open mouth and its chest. The thing falls dead.

"Damn it, Jack!" I yell.

"What?"

"You just alerted the others; you shouldn't have shot your gun."

"Shouldn't have shot my gun!" Jack yells, "Did you see that fucking thing? What was I supposed to do? Kick it?"

"Well, yeah," I say.

"Fuck," Jack says, "Can you get Alex down?"

I look at my right hand, then make a fist. I haven't used the power in a while; hopefully, it's strong enough to handle what I am about to do. The skin tightens as the scars squirm along my hand and forearm. I close my eyes and concentrate on my breathing, and not the toxic smell. I try to pull my mind into a field, one where Laura and I have hung out, had lunch while sitting on a blanket. Breathing in deep the smell of the flowers around us, the grass, the clean air. Again, I don't think this memory is real, or truly belongs to me. I never thought of us as picnic people, but it was there for me to pick from so I could use the power properly in a situation such as this. I hear a cracking noise; the web is coming apart, lowering Alex's unconscious body towards us.

"Shit!" Jack fires at another spider creature that was in the other room. It hurries across the ceiling, hissing angrily. It too drops dead, falling from the ceiling after taking three bullets to the rear. Jack fires one more into its head when it squirms. "Had to make sure," he says as he pops out the clip, and quickly reloads it.

I grab a hold of Alex, careful not to let the unscarred parts of my body touch the poisonous material. I can still feel it, but not as much with my right hand. Once I tighten the flesh and focus on the power I have, the poison does not affect my skin as much. We need to hurry since I don't know how long I can do this, but also for fear of being overrun by the spider creatures.

I yell for Jack to follow, as I am hauling Alex, one handed, towards the door. Jack fires on two more spiders coming from the other room, this time only using a bullet per creature as he gets perfect head shots, killing them instantly.

"That's how you shoot!" I say, not able to help myself busting his balls and trying to find some humor in our current situation.

He points the gun in my direction and fires. The head of a spider creature explodes, killing it instantly. It falls from its place on the door frame. I kick it aside.

"Thanks," I say.

"Just making sure I continue to impress your ass."

Our little gun fights in Alex's apartment have alerted the others. They have broken through the fabric of reality. The building is now crawling with these things, as they make their way towards us. As I am dragging Alex with my right, my left takes aim. First shot I miss, head feeling slightly woozy as I continue to touch the webbing. Once I regain my focus, the next bullet takes out the spider creature.

When we reach the bottom step, we fire on the creatures that have made their way off the building and are now scurrying toward us. These two are the size of a large dog; their teeth gnash, and their arms wiggle for purchase. The arms dispatch from their bodies when met with our bullets. They go down. More come at us; the place is infested. The next batch isn't that close to us. I open the passenger door, kick the seat aside and throw Alex's body into the back seat one handed. I fight the heroin in my veins; the world is wavering. I shake my head to place things back in focus.

"Give me the keys," I say to Jack.

"Are you out of your fucking mind? You almost had a panic attack earlier and now you look high as a kite."

"What I need to do to heal me and Alex only I can do, trust me."

"Damn it." Jack scrowls, takes the keys out of his pants pocket and drops them into my open hand. Now he's firing on another assault of those things, while I make my way to the driver's side.

We both get into the car, and I start it. Already, the roar of her engine is helping. Even though I feel the onset of the panic attack returning, I fight it. Memory comes to me like a mist clearing and I am shifting gears and working the clutch like I had just done this yesterday. She lurches forward; a few of the smaller spider creatures get caught under her tires, and she crushes them.

I shift again, bringing the car to high speeds.

"Whoa, what the fuck are you doing we're going to hit that— "

The muscle car drives through the building like it was never there in the first place. The world shifts. The ground has rough terrain and spreads open in all directions. The mountains I've seen other times are far on the horizon. We can drive on this land for a long time, which is good. We need to do that to ensure Alex's health returns, as well as my own.

"Wow." Jack breaths while he surveys his surroundings. "This is it, huh? This is what's causing all the weird shit."

"Yes," I say, "This is the Red Plane."

6.

"How's Alex looking?"

When we had first crossed the threshold after our battle with the spider things, Alex had gone into seizures from the heroin overdose from the web.

I've been driving us for a while, whatever a while is in this world. To me, it felt like ten, fifteen, maybe twenty minutes. I'm not going to lie though, I'm enjoying driving through this section of the Red Plane, as desolate as it is. The heroin that was surging through my body from the spider web is mostly gone. My head is still a little light, but I don't feel high. I'm hungry.

Jack reaches in the back seat, checks Alex's pulse. "Better. Alive. Not out of the woods yet, but his seizures have stopped. His breathing is regular, and he has stopped foaming at the mouth. So, this place can actually heal him?"

Figures come into view on both sides of the car. They start to come closer.

"Some kind of animals," I say.

"Look at these things," Jack says, amazed.

The animals running alongside my car are the size of a baby elephant, but have the body of a wart hog. The manes that runs along their heads and backs are spikes that look sharp. I don't see any eyes but the faces are covered in a multiple array of tusks. The bodies are covered with small mouths, and the tails are tentacles with tiny hooks that stick out of each suction cup that lines the inside of it. They don't have hooves like a normal war pig; the feet have three digits, with black talons.

They start to come closer to the car. I stop Jack before he rolls down the window and fires on them.

"It's just a herd," I say. "I don't think they will attack; they are just doing what they are meant to do."

"And what's that?"

I don't have an answer for Jack, because, really, I don't know. I'm not an animal expert, especially about the ones in this place. They just didn't seem threatening to me. There's another emotion in the way they are acting.

"I think they are scared of something."

As I say that, one of the mutant hogs nearby gets trampled on. Whatever it was causes the hogs to tumble over each other. The trampled one is left behind in a cloud of dust. I think I notice the other creature ripping into the mutant hog. Then more of the other creatures start charging in. I immediately know what they are when I get a clear view. They have the same features as the ones back at my house, dark scaly bodies with long arms and legs.

"Shit, it's the damn blood hounds."

"The what?" Jack asks.

"Those things we heard about when we first met The Dead One. They hunt down people if they don't pay a debt or race a wager. They attacked me earlier, too."

"Oh," Jack says, "Can we shoot those things at least?"

"No, don't waste your bullets, not yet." I shift gears and push the speed past one hundred. We've been on this terrain for a while, and I'm not sure if there are cliffs up ahead. I'd hate to run out of ground, while going at this speed, with creatures hunting other creatures around us.

More hogs go down. One gets close, avoiding the blood hound that runs up to jump on its back. Frightened, the hog swipes its multi horned face into the side of my car. I fight to keep control of Midnight Beauty, trying to steer clear of this hog only attacking in defense, while trying not to drive into others from the herd. Time is running out. If Alex doesn't wake up soon, I can see this going bad in so many ways. I'd hate to go back to our world when he's not fully healed. then we would have another situation to deal with. Midnight Beauty covers two more miles of desolation with the horde still keeping up with us. Another pack of blood hounds are charging in for the kill, and they are coming fast.

Finally, Alex stirs awake and starts coughing.

"Hey, hey man! You alright?"

He pops up from behind the seat, smiles at me, then throws his head behind Jack's seat and throws up. Jack winces. When Alex is done wretching, he sits up. He puts his head between the seats again; his eyes are feverish, and he's pale, but I think he's good enough to go through a wormhole. Now we just need to find one.

"Randy?" he asks, his voice is hoarse.

"Yeah, it's me buddy. Here to save you," I say.

"What the hell took you so long?"

"We were occupied, man," Jack adds, "Not like you weren't wrapped up or anything."

"Oh," Alex says, "We are funny all of a sudden. I see how it is." He looks out the windshield. "Holy shit, is this the Red Plane?"

"Yep," I answer. "We're not going to be here long; we have company."

Alex turns around, his eyes are wide when he looks at us again. "What the hell are those things?"

"Long story," Jack says, "But they are nothing compared to the company you had in your apartment. I think you may have to reconsider who you have over to your place."

Alex chuckles. "Right, sure. Enjoy the smell of vomit behind your seat, asshole."

"You're cleaning that when we get out of here," I add. In all honesty, I am hoping it'll clean itself up.

One of the blood hounds' leaps onto the hood; it stands in the middle of the windsheild hissing. We all scream collectively. I swerve the car left, then right, trying to shake the thing off. It's head splits open, revealing the vertical rows of teeth lining the sides. A tentacle lashes out and strikes the windsheild. It retracts, then hits it again and again.

I can't shake the damn thing off my car. Jack jumps up in his seat, pointing ahead.

"There! Right there! Wormhole! Get us the hell out of here!"

Up ahead, where Jack is pointing, there's a wormhole swirling on the surface of the nearest mountain. I turn toward it, while the creature on my hood continues its onslaught against my windshield. I grit my teeth as a crack appears. No, I don't care if it gets in. I can kill it with my bare hands. I'm mad that my car is taking damage after just getting her back.

The thing is still holding on as we drive into the wormhole. Surprisingly, it hasn't dissolved into nothing, or lost its grip on my car. Its black talons hold onto the lip of the hood. I turn on the windshield wiper blades; they go back and forth, striking it in the face numerous times. The vertical mouth and tentacle go after it, only to be met with a face full of windshield washer fluid. It screeches while all three of us laugh at it.

Midnight Beauty exits the wormhole; we are now in a wooded area. Tires cut into dirt. I down shift and hit the brakes. The creature loses its grip and is flung off the hood. It hits the ground, rolling over a few times before coming to a stop. It gets up, hisses at us again, and gets into position to charge at my car.

Rapid fire cuts through the air; the creature dances sporadically as its riddled with bullets. It falls dead. The bullets strike the ground in front of the car. Bullet holes appear in the hood as the shooter aims at my car.

"Get down!"

The three of us duck down as the windshield explodes, bullets whiz by our heads. One hits the head rest of Jack's seat. I'm afraid to look to see if he was hit, but he looks ok, hands over his head in cover. Alex has his body squeezed between the front and back seats.

The gun fire stops. The shooter must be reloading.

I open the car door and get out of the car, using the door as a shield in case the shooter is ready to unload another round on us. I tell Jack and Alex to get out of the car and take cover. Up ahead, I see a trailer; one of the windows is open. I close my eyes and focus; when I open them, a rock the size of my fist flies through the window. I hear a grunt as the shooter is stunned.

"Will!" I yell, "It's me, Randy! I have Jack and Alex with me! Stop shooting at us."

I honestly am not sure if it's Will who's shooting at us. If I think about what the Eye of Beholder told me, and the order our cars were in at the shop, then we must be at Will's trailer. We are met with silence. I am happy with the small break. Between the attack from the creature and then the gunfire, I haven't had time to truly think. Twigs snap; something moves quickly, in the woods, to the right of us.

I point, in that direction, to Jack. His handgun is in his hand, but he doesn't have time to bring it up. A tall man comes out of the woods with an automatic rifle. I recognize Will, even though he's in army fatigues and his head is shaved bald. It's the brown eyes and the bushy eyebrows; his long face hasn't really changed either, maybe a few lines from aging, other than that it's him.

"Damn, dude," I say holding up my hands, "You move fast."

Will aims the automatic rifle at my head.

"Don't move."

"Come on, man." I say taking a step forward. "It's me, Randy. I can't be that ugly that you can't recognize me."

"Don't fucking move!"

I shouldn't be surprised he would be living out here, in the woods, in a trailer, and dressed the way he is. He's always been a conspiracy freak, even in high school. The big one was that he was a believer that Tupac was still alive. He never let that go either, even as we got older. The attacks on 9-11 didn't help his mental state. He spun deeper and deeper into the rabbit hole of theory after theory. We entertained his theories for fun, especially when we went out drinking.

"Will, we don't have time for this, just put down the gun and— "

He pulls the trigger.

Even though I have healing powers, I don't know how I could survive a head shot. I duck, as quickly as I can, the moment he sprays the gunfire.

He wasn't aiming at me.

The blood hounds squeal when the bullets strike them. I turn around, a few fissures are open throughout the woods. The creatures fall, more come out of the fissures. I pull out my snub nose. Jack is aiming his handgun. All three of us are firing at the emerging creatures. Once they all fall dead, the fissure closes.

Will walks up to one of the dead creatures and spits on the carcass. "Fucking illuminati."

I open my mouth and then close it. Deciding it is best not to correct him.

He looks at me questionably. "How the fuck did you do that?"

"Do what?"

"Appear out of nowhere like that?"

"Come on, Will. Get your head out of your ass, you know what's going on. We talked about it after seeing Randy at the hospital," Jack says.

"Oh." He stares at me.

I point at myself. "Not the illuminati."

He looks at Alex.

"What's up, buddy?" Alex asks.

Will nods to him. "Yo."

He slings his rifle over his shoulder and walks away. I look at Jack. He shrugs.

"You guys coming or what?" Will asks.

"Where we going?" I ask.

"I was cooking dinner before you assholes rudely came out of nowhere. Don't worry, I'll still feed you."

Will walks over to a large grill, pulls the cover over, and smoke pours out. The sweet smell of barbeque fills the air. I salivate. My stomach rumbles. I look up to the sky, past the trees; this is the first time I see blue, and normal puffy clouds. Far into the distance though, there's a hint of red. This place has not been as badly affected as the few realities I've visited. We have time. We do need to eat though, to keep up our energy.

The ribs are delicious. I devour a whole rack and a chicken breast, relishing the flavor as I lick off the sauce, feeling I could take my fingers with it. At first, I was hesitant to drink any beer, but I do it anyway. I drain the first one quickly and release a healthy belch. We all need this, to feel some sort of normalcy, to have something that reminds us of our world, something we all enjoyed together. I think about what the beholder said about the testimony of truth. I would imagine it meant trust, or a gathering, like breaking bread, to bring our group back together again.

    I sit by a bonfire with my old friends, drinking cold beer and eating awesome barbeque. We talk of old days, high school and the best part of our racing days. Good memories. We all seem to remember things that we haven't or couldn't before. Maybe it's because we are together; our collective brains brought positive energy. We can focus on memories that were real to us. But our faces grew grim when it came to Chris and Cody.

    "Man, the fucking wheelman jobs," Alex says, putting his face in his hands.

    "Raise your hand if you had to kill someone from a racing gang because of a job Chris had given us."

    I raise my hand. Then Will. Then Alex. Jack is hesitant; finally, he slowly raises his hand. Just the look on his face, the shame and embarrassment. Somehow, I know what happened. Even if my crew had made a pact to help me, Jack had had to go to New Hampshire to escape for a bit with his family, to get away from this madness so he could feel prepared to handle it once again.

"Well, this was fun and all," Jack says, "But I think it's time to get to business."

We all nod at the same time.

"Yeah, I hope Tupac is in the Red Plane, I got so much to ask him."

We all look at him, then start laughing.

"Get the fuck out of here," Alex says, eyes streaming with tears from laughing so hard.

Jack was on his back laughing.

I calm down and say, "I'm not surprised. You thought those creatures were part of the illuminati!" More laugher.

"Fuck y'all," he says, "Bunch of ball busters."

Somewhere there is an explosion, far out in the woods.

The laugher stops.

"That's one of mine," Will says as he stands up.

"You can do landmines, too?" Alex asks, jumping up and grabbing his stuff.

"Yup. We need to hurry." He walks to a spot nearby, reaches into the leaves and pulls on a handle, opening a storm door.

"Holy shit." Alex breathes. We all look down into the bunker.

"Wow," I say, "That's impressive."

"Better be. I see what you have in that bag, kid's play." Will laughs, "Come on, let's load up before we get out of here."

There's another explosion, while we scavenge through the shelves. The guys grab more automatic rifles. I grab an Uzi, wanting to stay with smaller weapons. I'm happy to find that Will has an extra case full of .38 bullets for my snub nose.

Quickly, we load up my car with everything. Such a shame, not just that the food and the good times are now tainted, but it's this place, so serene and peaceful, barely touched by the Red Plane. The sky is still blue, the clouds still full, like looking up into a painting. I want just a few more moments of this before we jump ship again.

Will speaks, pulling me out of my somber mood.

"Do any of you clowns know where the fuck my car is?"

We all laugh.

The explosions are closer when we finally get in my car. I see things moving between the trees in the woods. Midnight Beauty roars like the beast she is, and off we go, back down the dirt trail we came in on. The car speeds into the new wormhole that appeared for us.

The next stop The Deceiver, something about that places a sickening feeling in my stomach. When we exit the wormhole, we are back in my neighborhood. Only this time, in this version, it's untouched by the Red Plane. It looks like it did when I left it. Street lights are on, the night sky normal above our heads, the stars winking at us. I pull into the driveway to a new home.

7.

My heart is pounding in my chest. The light is on in the house. I see a figure pass the kitchen windows a couple of times. Thankfully, it's not a ghoulish thing from the Red Plane. It's a female figure.

Laura.

I didn't think she would be home. I didn't think any of the lights would work in that house. When I last left the desolated place posing as our home, it looked like no one had been living there for months, years. But there she is, moving back and forth throughout the house as if she had a purpose. It brought back the nights I would come home from working at the shop and she wasn't working nights at the hospital yet. I would see her in those windows, busy making dinner.

I push open the car door. As I place my boot on the driveway, the memory slowly fades. Alex has crawled out from the back seat and is standing beside me. His brow furrows as he studies the light from the windows. The whole house is lit up, welcoming. Warm.

"Great, Laura's home," Jack says. He walks around the front of Midnight Beauty and stands on my right side, which is itching madly. The pain level was a dull four, it's slowly escalating to peak agony.

Will pops open the trunk and reaches in for the bag of guns, his and the ones I scavenged from my basement.

"Leave them," I say.

Will's head peers around the side of the open trunk lid at me.

"You crazy?" He asks, "Something doesn't look right."

"I know but bringing in a bag of guns isn't going to help anything; we don't know which Laura we are getting. You might scare her."

"I don't give a fuck!"

"Will!"

He slams the trunk and approaches me. I wait for him to throw a punch. Instead, his tall body looms over me, face in a scowl. He pokes his finger into my chest.

"Have it your way, Jones. But, when the shit hits the fan and we are overrun, and have no way to defend ourselves, I'll be the one who told you so."

I look at his finger in my chest indifferently, then peer up into his face.

"Finished?"

He waves his hand at me, making a sound of disgust and walks away to stand next to Alex.

"So how do you want to do this?" Jack asks. He's peering into the open mouth of my garage. "It's obvious her car's not here; it's at the shop with everyone else's." His eyes move to the roof.

"Randy? Do you see that? That roof looks brand new, don't you think?"

He's right. When we had first moved in, the garage was on the list of things to repair. We had mainly focused on the inside before I had my accident. I highly doubt a new garage roof was on Laura's mind while I was incarcerated. There had been spots where the roofing tiles were missing, like it suffered from bald spots. Some other pieces had been barely hanging on; none of that was present. The shingles are brand new, and, now that I am noticing, so is the paint. I bet, if I were too look inside, it wouldn't have the disarray of weights and car tools scattered everywhere.

I sigh and push myself off my car.

"Ok, let's go get her."

The steps did not creak and moan under our feet; these too are brand new. The wood still smells of the stain used on it. The door does not screech open. I walk into a completely different home.

My stomach feels like I got punched. I don't breathe for a long time. When I returned home before, it had been in ruins. None of that is present in this version. Everything, and I mean everything, is brand new. Instead of the ripped couches riddled with mold, this new one nearly stretches across the length of the living room, the attachment of the L shaped couch bent at the other side of the wall.

The wide screen television is easily a 70 inch, it owns most of the wall across from the couch. The coffee table is a nice glass one. The dining room table is the same but the wood looks like it has been polished multiple times. The colors of the walls are warm; they make the entire house look alive with the colors of yellow and blue. Not the grayish colors the walls were before. The stair case is new wood, still it's original color, not stained yet like the front steps.

This is what our home would've looked like had I not raced that night. Instead I had gone against Laura's wishes. She was done with the life; I should've been, too. God, or the forces that be, whatever choice of names you want to give the divine, knew too well I should have been done with that life. It had drained me of my human qualities; Still I hungered for the thrill, the challenge. Cody challenged me, and I complied without thinking twice. Laura was ready to spend days snuggled on the couch after work and binge TV shows all night, go to sleep and start all over. She wanted a family, even though she knew I had blood on my hands. I was not ready; I remained the blood thirsty beast. I did not want to be caged, but I ended up caging myself.

I hear humming coming from the kitchen. Laura's voice. I can't recall if I had ever heard her project a harmonious and beautiful sound. Something strange occurs to me; the song she is humming reminds me of a lullaby. I don't know how or which one, maybe it's just my subconscious. Possibly, the Red Plane is cherry picking other versions of our lives. She walks out of the kitchen, only comes as far as the dining room when she stops. She sings to the bundle of blankets cradled in her arms a few seconds longer before she pulls her face from it to look up at us. I swallow hard.

Her face lights up with a big smile. "Hey, Honey! I didn't hear you walk in." She's eyeing the guys behind me, the smile wavers, just a little, the corners of her mouth begin to drop, only to pull at the cheek bones again. "And you brought company! What's up guys? It's been a while. I didn't make dinner tonight, and you know Randy, doesn't tell me everything." She brings her attention back to the bundle in her arms. "I can order pizza if you want."

Laura makes cooing noises and wiggles her nose at the bundle, her body bounces back and forth. The bundle giggles. Tiny hands reach out to her as Laura leans in to give motherly kisses. I want to throw up. I want to die right here where I stand. This can't be happening; there is no way she is holding our child. Laura had lost the baby while I was in the burn unit, healing after the accident.

My jaw works uselessly, trying to find the words to say to her. I can't think; the muddiness is back and all I see is this new house, ridden of the stains of the past. I see my smiling wife, yes, she is my wife this time. I see the wedding ring sparkling on her left hand. I see our baby, alive and well, her lively sounds are heaven. This is all I see in front of me and nothing else. This is all I want.

Heart fluttering, my wife makes her way to me with our child. I feel my friends stir uncomfortably behind me, but it feels like they are far away. They're not even in this house. It's just us. My family.

I see the baby's soft skin wiggle within the confines of the blankets. Laura helps the infant's struggles by peeling a little away, revealing the small round head coated with light brown hair. The new baby smell is wonderful; it's mixed with the scent of shampoo. Laura must've just given the baby a bath, which would explain why the baby is still naked. The overprotective father in me wants to tell Laura to cover the baby so it doesn't get sick.

"Boy or girl?" I ask. I bring my hand, my left hand, up to touch the soft skin; the baby is real. It giggles, the small hand grips my finger.

"Girl." Laura says, her eyes are wet.

She's acting like this is the first time we have reunited. It would make sense since I was in jail and had just been released. No. That doesn't make sense; My little girl would be two years old by now. But the way Laura was acting when we came in was like she was waiting for me to come home from work. What the hell is going on?

"You want to hold her?"

I don't know what to say. I don't say anything; I just hold out my shaking hands.

"Randy," Jack says. "Don't. This isn't real, man."

Laura looks at him with daggers in her eyes. When she looks at me, she's smiling again. "Of course, this is real, sweetie. This is all we worked hard for. Didn't you want this?"

"Yes… Yes. Of course." What would it feel like to hold my daughter? To feel her small body wiggle in my arms, her warmth against my chest?

A hand gently lands on my shoulder. For a moment, I thought it might be Grandpa's hand, which confuses me. Grandpa would only place his hand on my shoulder when I was distressed, when I was losing control. I can't be losing control when I finally understand what true happiness is like. Can I?

It's not Grandpa's hand, but Jack's. He's starting to agitate me; he's taking my moment away from me. I fight closing my hands into fists. I want my baby in my hands, but I cannot bring myself to take her from

Laura's hands, and she's not lowering the baby into them either.

"Randy," Jack says, "Listen to me. Listen to us. Don't take the baby. She's not real, none of this is real. This is the Red Plane feeding off your regrets. You said it yourself, the house was in shambles when you first came here. How did it everything become new so quickly? Think man."

"Yeah, Randy," Alex adds, his hand on my right shoulder, "Fight this."

Will joins them. His hand is on my left shoulder with Jack's, "You got this, bro."

I almost shake their hands off me when I see Laura's face change from pure happiness to a mask of pure disgust. It makes me feel disgust at her and the writhing thing in her arms. I imagine myself reaching into the blanket, wrapping my hands tightly around the small head--

Stop. This is madness.

The house shudders. The walls groan as cracks slowly appears in the newly painted walls. Deep in the catacombs of my home, a baby wail. It did not come from the baby in front of me; this sound was distant, lost and sorrowful. My body trembles, the walls are peeling.

"Randy," Laura says intensely, "I don't like your friends disrespecting me in our home." Her neck cracks as it bends to one side, her skin slowly turns to an ashen gray. The bright warmness of the inside of the house dims to the color of blue flesh.

"You going to hold the fucking baby or what?" Laura barks, her voice guttural.

My hands turn to fists. My pain level is a motherfucking ten. I back away from the thing Laura has become. This is not some alternate timeline where I can leave all the shit I've done behind and live a happy and fulfilled life. This is the house of illusions, and it just had me in its maw, like a Venus fly trap. I just hope I can save her like I saved the others.

The blanket in Laura's arm is soaked in blood.

"Holy fucking fuck," Alex says, "That's not good."

"Yo," Will says, "The windows are flashing red; I think we are merging again."

For the first time since this journey started, I am truly afraid. I could fight thousands of blood hounds and Nazi's to the death, and fucking smile while I was doing it. But this. This is my true nightmare come to life, all my hopes and dreams turned on me. This isn't just Laura's Red Plane, this is mine as well.

"I think I see those things running towards the house," Will says, "I told you we shouldn't have left the fucking guns! But no one listens to the crazy conspiracy guy!"

"Shut up, Will," Alex screams, "You're not helping!"

The baby snarls. The bloodied blanket falls from it. as the small body thrashes around, revealing flesh the same deathly blue color as the spoiled walls of the house. Scales cover the baby from head to toe. Her fingernails are tiny black talons. The eyes don't look at me with the recognition of a child for a parent; they are cold and full of dread. Laura is smiling maddingly now, a smile I've seen too many times on the ghoulish faces of this plane.

"You won't take her, fine. She'll come to you," Laura says.

The thing leaps from Laura's hands and lands on my chest. My vision is full of those tiny black talons and a tiny mouth full of teeth. I suffer lacerations to my face, hands and arms as I try and fight off the dead baby's attack. It's little body scampers along my body, evading me swiftly every time I make a grab for it. I dance around, like a lunatic, trying to shake it off me. Alex and Jack are nearby, unsure how to proceed. Alex throws a punch, missing the creature entirely, striking me on the side of the head. I stumble back.

"Watch what you're doing!" Jack yells at Alex.

"I don't see you fucking trying anything," Alex yells back.

The dead baby climbs to my shoulder, perching there just long enough to screech at Alex, then turn the tiny mouth on me, taking a bite out of my neck.

I scream as the razor-sharp teeth tear into my flesh. I grab hold and yank it off my shoulder. It squirms violently in my hands as I squeeze. I don't feel the pain as its teeth and claws tear into my fingers and my hands. I want to squeeze until its fucking brains pop out of its head. This creature, posing as my unborn child, feeding off my fears and guilt, gluttonously fills me with such anger that my scars go into an insane fury of a flare up. Its eyes bug out from its small head as I continue to squeeze, then, with my right hand, with all the might my power will allow me, I slam its body to the floor. It explodes like a porcelain doll. I swear I can hear the fragile glass shattering upon impact. My vision grows dark around the edges. I don't think it got a major artery, but it's enough damage that the blood from the wound has run down and soaked most of the right side of my shirt. I need to heal myself soon or all of this will be for nothing.

Chaos erupts around me. The wide screen TV to my left is shaking crazily from its place on the wall; the attachment is a neck with pulsing black veins. The screen explodes, then pushes outward until a round head breaks through. The scaly creature has no eyes; its head splits open into a mouth; three or four appendages slither out and sniff the air. The blood hound screeches as it slowly climbs out of its imprisonment. The sound is met with numerous screeches outside the house.

Alex and Jack advance on the one coming out of the TV. The creature doesn't get a chance to lash out at them, as they are able to get their hands around the thing's neck and pull downward. There's a tearing sound as the flesh is severed from the shards of the TV, decapitating the head from the body.

"I hear them," Will says, "But, I don't see them." The world flashes red outside. "Oh fuck, there they are!" Then it flashes back to normal. There's a grave look on his face. "There're a lot of them."

"Kitchen," Alex says, "There have to be knives in this house."

"This house is fake as fuck!" Will yells, "We're not going to find anything useful in here!"

I'm trying to yell to them, but the words won't come to my mouth. Where's Laura? I haven't seen her since she let the dead baby loose on me. The house flickers, leaving me in a split second of darkness. When I can see again, Laura is there, smiling.

I feel the knife plunge into my stomach.

"Laura?"

Her face almost becomes sympathetic, almost. Her hand caresses the left side of my face. There's no comfort in her touch; the sadness in her eyes is full of mockery.

"I'm sorry, sweetie, I am really am. But you brought this upon yourself; you brought this upon us." She stabs me again. This all seems so familiar. My knees grow weak, wanting to crumble beneath me.

It's familiar because it's the same type of weapon the Nazi's used against me back at the prison. I thought, at first, they were just shanks, nicely made. Now I've come to realize that's not true; the weapon with the tentacle wrapped around its crimson color hilt has been made with a purpose.

I fall forward when she twists the knife in my stomach. She whispers frantically in my ear. I've heard these words before. I don't understand any of the syllables of the dead language, but one word, just one word, I remember. The last Nazi I killed, the big guy, had tried to say something while I held his guts in my right hand. I recognize it the moment it slithers from Laura's mouth.

"Alter Inhorruit."

She steps away. The knife is withering. I look down at it to find that it's the tentacle on the hilt that's withering, pulling free from the wood. It slowly moves forward, entering my body. The hilt starts to disintegrate, turning into gray ash, then disappears completely as if blown away by a small breeze.

Laura crashes to the floor, tackled by Alex. Jack runs over to me. His hands are on my shoulders; he's speaking but the words are muffled. I look over to Laura. She's not fighting Alex; she's laying still, face unreadable. Except for the single tear trailing down her cheek.

Fissures rip into the walls. Jack leaves me, kitchen blade in hand and attacks a blood hound trying to get in from one of the fissures in the foyer. The fissure closes once Jack impales the side of the creature's head with the knife, killing it. The foyer is back to normal, creature dead and gone. Alex leaves Laura where she lay, probably realizing she's not going to do anything and he's better suited joining the fight. He and Will kill a couple of creatures in the dining room; those openings close shortly after. The house is shaking; there're far too many of them for my three friends to handle.

A blood hound enters from a fissure that no one has noticed. The creature sneaks out of the fissure, crawling on all fours, and makes it way to me.

I try to move. I try to heal myself. Ever since the tentacle entered my body, and Laura spoke those words, my right side is cemented, not allowing me to move it. I can move my left side freely; I pull forward. It's like pulling dead weight. Sweat breaks out on my forehead. I try to close my right hand, to call upon the gift I have been cursed with, but I feel nothing. I feel the scars. They move freely while still attached to the right side of my body. The itching and burning drives me to insanity.

"Don't worry," a voice says inside my head, "You don't need to keep fighting. It'll all be over soon."

I remember the voice. I heard it before, when I first entered my house. I heard it when the scars in my reflection talked to me before I had set out to save my friends.

The fighting is still going. I hear Alex yell they are outnumbered. I fall to my knees. The world is slipping from me.

My front door opens.

8.

    Pain level is infinity. My body is trembling and drenched in sweat. The worst part of this whole ordeal is my right side. The scars are alive. This feeling of absolute hopelessness is equally as torturous as having the world decay within me while I was in prison. All I want to do is keep moving, keep fighting. I am locked into place in the middle of my living room, one half of me defeated into exhaustion while the other half weighs me down while it tries to pull from my body.

  I don't need to look up to see who my visitor is because I can tell by the Converse on his feet.

  "Look at this!" he says excitedly. "The whole crew is here! Almost the whole crew." He chuckles. He places a large red item near me, the liquid sloshes inside. The smell of gasoline hits my nostrils.

  "Man, if I knew we were going to have a reunion, I've would've dressed for the occasion. Nah, fuck it, I wouldn't have."

  He kneels, so he's face to face with me.

  "Not looking too hot, Randy boy."

  I didn't feel too hot either. My body shivers uncontrollably; the chills give me the sensation of icicles growing inside my body. Despite feeling like absolute shit, I can't help but get in a reply to Chris.

"You don't look so good yourself, asshole."

At this point, the guy could be a walking corpse. There's a bruise on his face, an ugly spot of rot that's a purplish green, and it looks like it's spreading. While most of his skin is taut and tightly stretched across his skull, that one spot is an empty crater, the cheek bone parts of his jaw showing.

He makes his tsk tsk tsk sound. His tongue clacking against his teeth is a grating sound; it sends a wave of pain and annoyance through my brain. I wish I could hit him in that same spot, watch with satisfaction as half of his face collapses.

"Always defiant till the end. I wish I could've seen you at your weakest point in your life. At the hospital, suffering from your burns. I would've been there by your side, if we were still friends, but you had to take everything so fucking personal." He cocks his head upward, closes his eyes and inhales deeply. "I can smell the despair, so much it covers your tough guy bullshit."

I force a smile. When my lips move on my right side, it feels like the scars are fighting the movement.

"Let's see how long you can hold that smile after I get my hands around your neck and fucking snap it."

Chris sighs. Death rides on his breath.

He reaches into his back pocket. I flinch when I see the weapon.

His icy blue eyes smile within the black abyss of his sockets.

"I knew you would recognize this." He holds it out in the palm of his hand, showing the knife with the crimson handle and tentacle wrapped around it. "Don't worry, I'm not going to stab you, even though I would love to, multiple times, just for fun. Maybe cut out your tongue to finally shut you up." He points the blade at Laura, who hasn't moved since Alex tackled her during the attack. Her eyes are open, her breathing is steady, but there's nothing else of her. it's as if she's gone comatose.

"Your lovely girlfriend there already did what was needed. If anyone could do it, I knew it would be her. Not those idiot Nazis, but, then again, I don't think any of us knew you could use your right arm to rip through a body like it was nothing."

A blood hound crawls through the front door. I can see the Red Plane beyond. The world hasn't flickered between its existence and our world for some time now. I assume we are now fully covered, at least for the time being. Now these things don't have to rip fissures through time and space. They can just walk in, uninvited, no matter the outcome. It goes to Chris like a loyal dog, in its talons a statue. It's the statue that was at the bottom of the gun bag.

Chris places it in front of me, so I can see every detail of the vile thing. The elongated head shaped like a tusk, the shape goes downward, the point almost touches the back. On its back are wings, not expanded to the full size; although, if the real thing was in front of me, I would imagine those wings could stretch out to eternity. The body is lined with the faces frozen in their suffering. The design is supposed to be a representation of the Dead One in its true form. I been fortunate not to have witnessed it yet. I have only known The Dead One in his human form, which is sinister enough.

"How about this, recognize this beauty?"

"Yes," I say. Each word is now growing painful to say. I fight for breath. "It's what I am going to shove up your ass after I break your neck, or maybe the other way around, depending on how I feel."

Chris laughs. There's no humor in it, just mockery.

"Look around, Randy. You're not doing shit, and neither is your crew."

I turn my head. Laura is nearby in her comatose state. The blood hounds that are the arachnid shaped things from before have surrounded Will, Jack, and Alex and wrapped them up, confining them in their webbings. The things stay nearby, waiting for the word to pounce and rip them to shreds. Jack is squirming in his trap, trying to rip out of it. One of the hounds hovers over him, growling.

"Don't listen to him, Randy! You can get us out of this! We haven't lost yet."

"Oh, but you have, Jack." Chris replies, "You've lost big time brother. And, once I am done with your fearless freak of a leader, I'm going to make sure you are stuck in your nightmares, constantly watching, on repeat, your father's demise. I know your dreams, your father hanging from the hook that disemboweled him, his guts laying on the floor just inches away from his dangling feet. The other two will race eternally by your side, Randy. Slave to the wagers and their bets. And Laura, she's just fine with your baby and the house, the two things you never wanted."

Anger boils inside of me. It burns away the lock on my left arm, not completely, but enough for me to lash out. My left fist connects with his face. He jumps to his feet, holding his face. When Chris pulls his hand away, its smeared with blood. My body fights against me. I don't think I can throw another punch like that, but it's ok; I like what I see. Chris stares at the blood; he's not smiling anymore. For a second, I see the old him, the human side; there's regret in his eyes. Pain. As if the punch and the damage done woke something within him, but it only lasts for a second. He turns back toward me, the wound is ugly as ever now. When he smiles, I can see everything move inside of that hole.

"Alright, Randy. I get it now, we are not going to see eye to eye on everything. So, it's time to end this party and send everyone home." He grabs the gas can.

Images flash through my mind. The explosion replays over and over, a hot fiery cloud that surrounds my body. Then the hospital, those days of lying there, constantly clicking the morphine button as if it has gone dry and I have no choice but to continue living with the pain. I don't want to feel this again.

"Don't." I hate the sound of my voice. I can go down fighting, but this is too much for me to bare.

Chris ignores me, tips the gas can over, and splashes my body with the clear liquid. The smell of gas is overpowering. I shiver uncontrollably, teeth chattering.

"It'll all be over soon," the voice says. I assume the voice belongs to the Scarred One. The right side of my mouth moves as he talks.

"There he is!" Chris says, the excitement coming back in his voice, "Man, that is some freaky shit."

The Scarred One is attached to me; the entity is my scars, a living organism. Is he the reason why I have my powers? It would make sense since I had gained these abilities after the accident, after the burns had healed.

"Why are you doing this?" I ask The Scarred One.

"You are planning on ending me. You want to go to Death Highway and end all of this, end me. I don't want that. I want to exist. I deserve to exist. So, while I was born of the fire you created, I took a chance before you could even be aware of what was happening to you. I made a deal with the Dead One to release me from you. I will freely walk the Red Plane and you will be a slave to the wagers, eternally race for them. You have a lot of debt to pay, Randy Jones."

"Man," Chris says, "This is wild, to see you talking to yourself." He laughs. Then he takes off his shirt, showing his emaciated body.

The entire upper body is tattooed. I recognize the images. The same imagery of chaos and ritualistic sacrifice was on the Nazi's bodies in the prison. The only difference is Chris has the knife with the tentacle wrapped around its hilt tattooed on his chest, the point of the blade touches the place where the neck meets the breast bone. The tentacle tattoos are writhing on his chest as Chris continues to speak the strange chanting. It's all coming together now, this plan of insanity. I can't allow this to happen.

"You have no choice," The Scarred One says.

Chris sparks the match; it lights up his face like a crazed jack-o-lantern.

"Any last words, Randy."

My lips tremble as the left side of my mouth fights to form the words.

"Fuck. You."

The smile on Chris's face broadens. He drops the match. My body lights up; there's a whooshing sound, followed by the intense heat licking at my flesh. My vision engulfs in tidal waves of red. The Scarred One and I scream in union.

"You're journey ends now," Chris says. I can barely hear him, the roaring flames and searing of my flesh muffles his words. "When this is over, you'll be my bitch for all eternity."

The Scarred One awakens.

9.

The room is dark. It smells of dust and mold. I'm sitting in a chair that's supposed to be cushioned; its rocky surface makes my ass hurt. The wallpaper is a faded yellow, it's peeling. Shadows cover what's underneath. That's ok; I don't want to look anyway. The outdated flowers wither with the wallpaper. The bed is a gray tombstone. The small television flickers silver images of a little boy fixing cars with his Grandfather. He's on a step ladder; his small body leaning into the open hood of the car. He's tightening a part of the engine. I have seen this before. Why am I here?

"I like this program."

My head whips around. My mouth is a desert.

"Grandpa?"

The old man in the rocking chair does not turn to look at me. He's focused on the two figures on the screen; he's smiling. The past flickers in his far away gaze. The rocking chair creaks slowly like aching joints. I stare at him for a very long time, trying to figure out where the rest of him went. He has lost a significant amount of weight the past couple of years. I noticed it the last time we had spoken, during visiting hours. In the visitor area, there are heartless little booths that're supposed to make you feel like you have a connection with the outside world. You're divided between a plate of glass; a phone on both sides is the only form of communication. It's ridiculous when the person is right there, right there in front of you! Voices are consumed by the glass; the phone is a transmitter.

That was the day he told me my grandmother had died. She had suffered a heart attack. The doctors thought it was from the stress. She had spent many sleepless nights worrying about me. While I was suffering in the hospital, she was there. Even after we lost the baby, there was no judgement. She just wanted to see her grandson get better and be there every step of the way. I witnessed each day drain her soul. Her face was ten years older than the day before.

On the screen, Grandma is cooking our favorite Sunday breakfast, French toast and scrambled eggs. The boy is older, so is the man. They are laughing. It sounded beautiful, but, when they speak, the words are backwards. I can't understand them. It infuriates me because it's taking away the only moment we have left. My heart warms again when they are smiling and laughing. Static lines ripple up and down the screen momentarily, then they are gone.

Grandpa's cheeks are wet with tears. I put my head down. Defeat.

His hand shoots out, grip still as strong as I remember it, like he wasn't an old man battling dementia. His eyes are wild as they bore into me.

"Tell my grandson he needs to get his shit together. You're one of his friends, right? Tell him for me, will ya. The Wayfarer of the dead is corrupt; there's only purification and light."

He lets go and goes back to watching our memories on TV.

I can't find the words to speak.

"Tell him to just fix it! The universe is broken. Fix it!" he yells.

The shades pull open; the windows cast a landscape with a bleeding sky. The ground is cracked and fissured. Smoke is pouring out from beneath the ground of the strange plane. The Red Plane. I forget about it every time.

There's a figure hunched forward outside on the cracked ground. He's wrestling with himself, one half of his body is badly scarred. I look at my right side. I don't have any scars. Am I dead? Is this how I go to the other side, hanging out with my Grandpa first before I cross over.

Grandpa scoffs.

No, it isn't. Fuck that shit. I know exactly what's going on. I get out of the chair, give my Grandpa a kiss on top of his head, say nothing else and step outside. The air is hotter than normal in this world. I walk over to the struggling mass of flesh.

When one is suffering the throes of Purgatory, he faces pain and fire. His soul stills burn when he ascends. There's pain in purification and the light. And, hopefully, he who seeks redemption is granted it, instead of damnation.

10.

I walk along the fissures of time, into the burning darkness.

He's on his knees, the half of him that is human is not moving. The other half, where the scars cover most of his body, is writhing and pulling from him, detaching from its human host. I feel for this version of me, to go through life always in pain, always having to deal with how his body looks. He acts tough and fights through it; that's always going to be in his genes, that unwavering stubbornness. It's in all our genes, no matter what plane we are on, or universe we are a part of. I feel for him, even if he is the cause of his scars, of his pain. I am the cause of it.

Now he is a living host because of the Red Plane merging with his universe. Everything has an organic quality to it, like the demons of the dark are merging their own flesh to pass through, to own, to build their own foundation. To exist.

The only forms that are three dimensional are this Randy and the Scarred One. Closing in on them, through the burning pages of the illusion, I walk through the smoke. There's darkness behind these pages. I hear the things living there, stirring, grumbling; their slick and disgusting bodies sliding in the cold space, wanting, hungry, not for flesh to feast upon but to satisfy something else. Our insignificance allows them to rule us, to reprogram us. The wrongs in this dimension are attracting them, and it's spinning on its axis.

The things in the dark are getting impatient, the claws on the disfigured hands tear through the two-dimensional fabric. Other things squirm within the enveloping darkness. I am in slow motion. The Scarred One grunts as he's twisting and turning, the taut flesh now stretching. He's almost fully away from Randy, but he's still having to regrow other parts of his body, the half that wasn't his. I am not concerned with that. I need to fix this, get me out of my head. He's shuddering in despair; sweat drenches his skin.

The Scarred One quickly turns his head toward me, sensing me. He's already formed most of his head. He has a full chin and mouth; the other half of his face is forming before my eyes.

"Keep away!" it warns.

"What you're doing is wrong."

"Fuck off."

"What do you think is going to happen when you are free? You're going to roam the city, find a life amongst the damned and the vile? You think that's a way to live?"

"It's better than not existing! The other half of me is a selfish prick! He wants to end it all; it's not fair. I wasn't asked if I wanted to come into this world. I am the Scarred One; I am born of fire and, for that, my existence is painful, but I am existing. If he finishes Death Highway, I am no more. I can't allow such cruelty!" he goes back to releasing his body.

"Stop, right now. I can't allow you to do this."

"The fuck you can't."

An arm, insectile and elongated, reaches around the barrier out of the darkness. It comes close to Randy; it brushes his leg. I rush over there and stomp on it. The thing squeals and yanks back its appendage. I place my hand on Randy. He's shivering terribly, but his skin is hot, almost too hot to touch. He's still fighting. In the other world, he's burning, but the flame isn't fully consuming his body.

The Scarred One crawls on the ground now, detaching his leg.

I straddle the being, holding him down. Once my hands touch the taut flesh, he stops growing. He struggles against me, gritting his teeth.

"What are you doing? How did you do that?"

"I am the merger of one," I say, "I can't allow you to separate from yourself when there's so much at stake." I grab his head, preparing to break his neck.

"NO, wait!" The Scarred One Cries.

"Why?"

"I don't want to die. I won't fully die; my mind will know I am just dead flesh on another being. It's eternal torture! "

"How do I know I can trust you?" I ask.

"Do I have a choice?"

The darkness has almost fully consumed this reality. The things are pulling themselves from the darkness onto the space we occupy like we are on a platform, just floating in nothing. They surround us, a collage of mouths and appendages. One of the montrosities clutches the Scarred One and begins pulling him towards its opened mouth. He screams for help, trying to fight it off with his hand. I grab the appendage; the slimy flesh singes under my grasp, It pulls away.

"You see? They don't care about your so-called feelings, your existence or the deal you made with Chris and The Dead One. They too want to exist, to claim what has been forgotten, so tell me why I shouldn't break your neck to save us all."

The Scarred One is crying; the tears are white and pus like. "I'll do whatever, just don't kill me. I can help! I have knowledge of the things here, of this world!"

I nod. I know what I can do.

My hand traces down to his lower back. I turn him over and punch my hand through his flesh. The Scarred One screams in agony.

"This won't take long," I say. My hand finds purchase, gripping his spine. One good turn of the wrist, and I feel it snap within my grasp. I pull out my hand , shake off the blood and tissue, and one of the creatures grabs it and gobbles it up greedily.

The Scarred One wails in a way that even tugs at my heart; I am human after all. I feel empathy for any of the things that exist in this nightmare. I have one more thing to do. I step between Randy and the Scarred One. I take one more look behind me at the nursing home; its far away, but I can see Grandpa's face in the window, watching. He is smiling.

Feeling hope inside, I grab the Scarred One with one hand, the other Randy with the other and pull them towards me, to wear them. They meld to my flesh. I zip up the front to complete the process.

We are whole; I can feel Randy coming back from his despair, the voice of the Scarred One is just a tiny whisper in the chambers of our mind. The two-dimensional world is slowly rebuilding itself, fighting against the fire that burned it. The world is recoating the darkness, pushing the monsters into their void. The house comes into view; the fire is out. The look on Chris's face makes me smile.

"This can't be." Chris steps back away from me. His eyes wide with disbelief.

I rise, the fire rolls off my back. The flames slowly go out and are now ashes that I shake off. Once I am standing fully erect, head up high, I feel different. Almost at peace, but the need for violence is still there; it's controlled. All of it, just balls of energy inside of me, circling around the same axis. Controlled.

"Why didn't it work; it should've worked. You shouldn't be here; you shouldn't be you!"

"I am the Merged One, of the collided and the bringer of balance," both the Scarred One and I say at the same time.

I close my fist; I can feel it. An invisible energy radiates in my hand; the sensation goes down my entire right arm and up to the side of my face. The Scarred One sighs. I do, as well. It's an amazing feeling; I feel no pain. My body is hardly as tight as it used to be; pieces of light start dancing around my fist.

Alex, Jack, and Will are free. I can feel the necks of the creatures that were holding them break in my hand, even though I didn't touch them. More of the dark scaly creatures slip in. My house erupts into violence as the horde of creatures outside start climbing through windows and charge in from the front door. I hear the door in the kitchen break open, and then the sound of talons scraping against my tile floor as they charge in.

The ceiling cracks and splinters. I am pulling pieces of wood with my mind. Then those pieces of wood explode, sending shards of splintered wood in every direction, piercing the monsters in the eyes, and through the center of their heads. Multiple bodies drop. I hear the drawers fly open in the kitchen. All the knives left over sail through the air, killing the next small wave of creatures.

"We can't kill all of them this way," The Scarred One says. "You'll exhaust yourself." I focus on my car in the driveway, the trunk to my car pops open. The heavy bag flies in from outside, stunning any of the creatures that happen to be in its way.

"Now that's what I'm talking about!" Will yells. The three of them tear into the bag, grab their gun of choice and start emptying bullets into any of the blood hounds that pile in. I open my right hand. My snub nose wiggles from the bag and comes to me; only I catch it with my left and start firing as well. Every one of my shots are precise. Each bullet is a head shot. Their bodies fall. When I am out of bullets, I flip the cylinder open; using my mind, I direct all six bullets into the cylinder, reloading the gun. I snap it closed with the flick of my wrist and continue firing.

Chris is still up against the wall, eyes wide open in disbelief that his plan has failed. I am loving every bit of it and can't help wanting to save him for last. I want to savor this entire battle, savor his loss.

"Don't get too cocky," the Scarred One says in my head. "He's a sneaky one."

I run out again. I'm about to reload, with my fancy trick, when Chris pulls a gun on me.

"If I can't have the power, no one can."

There's a primal scream behind me. I turn to see Laura charging toward us. She has a knife in her hand; it's pulled back. The knife flies from her hand as she throws it forward. It spins through the air. I feel it just barely miss me, but it wasn't meant for me.

The knife hits its target, sticking into the center of Chris's head. He fires the gun. The bullet strikes the floor, and he crashes down, twitching where he lay.

"They're retreating!" Jack yells.

"Yeah, how do you like us now, suckers!" Alex yells out the window.

"Told you," Will says to me, but with a smile.

I smile back.

Then I look over to Laura. She's breathing heavily. Any hint of the person she was seems to be gone. Her eyes don't leave Chris's body. He twitches again, and mumbles something unintelligible. I can't believe he's somehow alive, but, then again, I was inside another world, slipping my body on like it was a costume.

"Damn," Alex says, "Someone put this asshole out of his misery."

Jack raises his gun and points it at Chris. Laura screams in that primal way again, giving me chills. She runs over to where Chris is laying near the front door. She brings her foot up and stomps on his head. Then again. And again. She continues to stomp on his head until it's nothing but brain and bones she must scrape off the bottom of her shoe.

I place my hand on her shoulder. "It's over, honey."

She turns on me and for a moment I thought she was going to hit me next. Instead, Laura embraces me. Her lips touch mine, and she's kissing me furiously. The kiss sends chills throughout my entire body. More electrifying than the insane power I had wielded earlier.

She pulls away, tears falling from her eyes.

"I am so sorry, I. That wasn't me."

"I know," I say to her. "I know."

She hugs me tightly. I breathe in her scent. For the first time in a very long time, I feel complete.

Now, it's time for us to find the Dead One and demand access to Death Highway.

Part Two
New Providence

11.

After the battle against Chris and the horde of otherworldly creatures, we jump into my car and take a ride through, hopefully, what could be the last wormhole. We need to grab the cars from the Autobody shop.

The looks on each face as they looked upon their vehicles was one that matched my own when I was reintroduced to Midnight Beauty. Once everyone was done reliving their lives, we began our plan of action. Since we have the statue now and will be able to challenge the Dead One to open Death Highway to us, we all decide to hit the very first Industrial Area, the one that began it all during the Dead One's racing circuit.

Before getting into his car, Jack looks at the body shop one more time, a melancholy look on his face. I clap him on the back.

"It'll be here when we get back," I say, "It'll be good as new, and so will everything else."

He sighs, never taking his eyes off the shop. "I hope so." He takes a few more minutes and then finally gets into his Dodge Challenger.

We start our engines; one by one, the beasts roar. Revving our engines all at once, we want the world of the Dead One and his followers to hear us coming, and our cars are baring teeth. We pull out of the lot, one by one, with me in the lead, followed by Laura, Jack, Alex, and then Will in the rear. I see them watching from their windows as we loudly drive by, defying the mundane and the law of this land.

It's like this throughout most of the neighborhoods, and then we reach the highway. It's an unsettling quiet, how deserted the highway has become. It's never been this quiet; even at three in the morning, there's usually a few cars, here or there, going for an early morning drive, or to jobs that require workers to come in much earlier than most of us. It was dead quiet, except for us; once again, we wanted to be heard as we roared collectively down the empty highway.

When we arrive at the old Providence Brewery Warehouse, that, too, we found was deserted.

This was where it had all started. The first Industrial area to hosts the races. This is where I had learned that the mythology of The Dead One maybe wasn't a myth after all. The crowd would place bets on the racers and reap the rewards if the racer won. If the racer lost, well, it depended on how high the wager was. It may be days later, but something would happen to the racer, especially if they chose not to race anymore. Sometimes it would be a freak accident, and sometimes it was something as simple as losing control of their car and suffering a normal accident.

But the whispers about Death Highway, those were worth paying attention to. Even if I have never really believed in them, I couldn't help but be curious. There were these two racers who had become worthy enough to enter Death Highway and race each other. One of them was badly riddled with cancer; he should've been on his death bed the way he looked, but here he was, racing. Well, he won and showed up just to be a spectator, cancer free and looking healthy as ever.

It was an endless cycle of winners getting whatever they wanted from this being, who was like a Jinn in so many ways. If they raced, placed their own wagers and fulfilled the others, they had a chance to have whatever they wanted.

What these lost souls didn't realize was it was feeding the Red Plane, which feeds on the mundane. The people that won slowly withered away anyway and became part of the forsaken world. Some say, maybe those racers weren't worthy in the first place. Some disagree.

I had performed in those races. My prize was always money, which went to the house and anything else Laura and I needed. I also went to these races because Chris had placed a price on my head, using me to get us out of a bad situation. After he had made a deal with the Dead One, a deal I was not involved with, the people who were after Chris ended up dead, or worse. The ones who had ended up dead were on the news. I had put two and two together.

I became Chris's cash cow to eternal life, because he knew I could win every race. But I didn't; I don't even think I technically lost, either. I guess an accident during a race is disqualification, but I'm not sure. Never been sure of the rules of this world, which is a risk that I would have never taken if this had been my choice. But, then again, I did like the money. It had made our lives so much easier.

Cody McLaughlin had been one of my best friends. I had known him since high school, along with Alex and Will. Jack was in the same mechanics class as us, but I had known Jack since I was a kid, since my Grandpa and his father were the best of friends.

Cody was always jealous of my winnings. Right about the time I was supposed to quit racing for Laura, he had challenged me. One more. Of course, I couldn't refuse, not because of my addiction to the need for speed, but, truth be told, you really weren't allowed to refuse.

The place had been packed with spectators. Cody and I had pulled up to the starting line, which was right under an enclosed walkway that connected the two old warehouses together. Our engines revved, the crowd cheered, and The Dead One stood off the side, his large muscular arms over his chest, covered in tattoos. He had pulled out a large horn, one you normally see on a Viking. He blew into it, signaling the race had started.

Tires squealed and we were off. Cody and I were the best out of our crew, but I was better. We were neck and neck at the start; when we had to take hard turns sometimes that would warrant one of us taking the lead over the other. We raced along the nearly deserted streets of the industrial area, trying to top each other to see who could go the fastest before having to take another turn.

When we approached the finish line, it was a straight shot. I shifted gears quickly, taking my car past one hundred and twenty. His car shifted and he nearly caught up. This is when one of us would use the NOS to boost our speed. My finger hovered over the button. I heard his exhaust make the whoosh sound, he'd pressed his button. I had done the same. My car lurched forward, burying the needle; my body was compressed into my seat.

Then somehow, someway, for the first time ever in my racing life, I lost control of my car. I jackknifed to the right, into Cody's path; we collided into each other and then my car was tumbling over and over, the sound of shrieking metal in my ears. I blacked out for a short period of time. When I came to, I was hanging upside down. I struggled as I got my pocket knife out of my jacket. I pulled it open and cut the seat belt. I crawled out of my car, through broken glass. Other than being upside and slightly totaled, my car was fine. No gas leak, no signs of any other danger.

Cody's car was on fire.

I fought to get to my feet and hurried over to his blazing vehicle as fast as I could. My leg was all messed up from the accident, but I fought against it to save my friend's life. All those stupid fights over nothing but money and fame, and there he was, in his car, which was on fire.

I tried to pull him out. The fire carried over from his screaming body to my right side. I was still pulling even though my arm was engulfed in flames and it was creeping up to the right side of my face. Then his car exploded, and I was sailing through the air.

You know the rest.

Those memories surge through me as we drove slowly by the old area.

"No one here," Jack said over the radio.

But there was someone. In a very familiar black muscle car. It's covered in flames, as it races through the deserted areas of the industrial building. The fire shoots out from his car on all sides, consuming everything around him. I see his smiling face, the thing he has become since joining The Red Plane. The tires sound like the screeching of a thousand tortured souls. He doesn't leave until the whole place burns down. There was no point to it really; he just wanted me to know he was there.

"Who the hell was that?" Alex asks over the radio.

I grab the microphone from the radio overhead. "That was Cody."

12.

"We must go through the city; I'll be everyone's guide,' The Scarred One says.
The Scarred One tells us what to expect when entering the city. It's not the city we are used to; it's constantly changing as The Dead Ones are rebuilding it to suit their world. The buildings are meant to serve as barriers, like a radio transmission, once turned on they can come and go as they please, between our world and theirs.

"There will be chaos because chaos serves them well." The Scarred One says, "Then there's the cult."

"A cult?" Jack asks.

"Yes. They will stand in the middle of the street and allow other vehicles to run them down and kill them."

"That's messed up," Laura says.

"They believe it serves their Gods," The Scarred One continues, "Especially if the drivers are racing one of The Dead One's circuits, and even more gloriously if it's for Death Highway. They believe they'll come back to a better life. If you don't run them down, they become agitated very quickly and are known to attack in one collective mob.

"Lovely." Alex throws his head onto his car, already feeling defeat. "Just lovely. And what do you suggest we do about that, oh great Scarred One?"

I can feel my right-side squirm offensively.

"Just drive toward them," Scarred One says.

"Yo, that's fucking suicide," Will says.

"I wouldn't mind going out in a blaze of glory." Jack adds.

I smile at Jack.

"Seriously. I can help. Trust me." The Scarred One says.

"Ok." I say. "Let's do it guys; I trust me, him, whatever."

We get in our cars and slam the doors at the same time.

"Wouldn't want it any other way," Will says over the radio, "One last run with the best friends I could ask for."

Alex sighs, "Same here."

"Ditto," Laura adds.

"Enough of this shit, let's do this," Jack says this time.

"See you guys on the other side," I add.

I revved my engine. They all do the same. The collective sound of a pack of wolves, ready to run together, to hunt together, to end it all together.

"One last race, last one to the finish line faces an angry mob of suicidal cultists." I say over the radio.

The radio is silent, the revving of the engines is the answer I need. Tires spin, the sound a thing of beauty. I purposely burn rubber a few more seconds, just to let it last for a moment. It's not like my dreams, empty and hollow. The others are ahead by a few seconds. I'm off. I get some nice hang time with the front tires, the engine rips happily, ready to go to war. I look in the mirror, skid marks. I smile. If this world is still standing after our mission, I hope the monument is there forever, reminding whoever roams this forsaken place, you don't fuck with Randy Jones and his crew.

Their cars are evenly spaced, not much of a gap separating them from each other. I cover the distance, roaring right by them. The Scarred One laughs like a child. I know my car has been worked on more than theirs and it's because of Jack and his father that it's faster than ever before, but I can't help but be cocky. I have the same old competitive must always win attitude. My prize is bloodshed.

"Always got to be a show off," Laura chimes over the radio.

"Fuck that," Alex says, "We let him win, he was too busy dropping the soap in prison to be able to drive like he used to."

Laughter barks over my head. I smile. The Scarred One smiles. We smile collectively.

"You should lead anyway," the Scarred One says, "they are in for a hell of a ride, they'll need you to be the beacon. It's always been you."

"We," I say, "We should lead. Till the end."

Till the end.

No action yet as we enter the city, the sign reads: Welcome to New Providence. We slow our vehicles down, driving the normal speed limit to survey the strange new place growing on our world like an expanding mold.

"New Providence," Alex snickers, "The Dead One and his followers are colonists."

More laughter from the others. It dies down quickly when we drive further into the city. I take a turn on a street that used to be familiar but curves madly, like it belongs deep in the woods instead of being one of the main roads of a normal city. The whole place is twisting and turning from the shimmer coating everything.

I don't need to hear over the radio the collective sigh from all us. The sigh of the world. It's a very long pause before she breathes again. Time is fading away; I'm waiting for the final moment. Will we become slaves of this place or will we wink out like the hands of space slap together, squashing us in between like the tiny fly that we are. A pest, a nuisance, our purpose to wallow in the trash of a world we don't deserve. We will lay our larva, lay our disease; it will hatch, and we will multiply. Repeat the process. We will become a writhing mass of nothing.

"Randy." Laura's voice is small like a child. She pauses; I wonder if she sees what we all see, the figures moving up and down the buildings quickly, scurrying like ants. Each area of the building becomes something different, as if they are constructing it to a new look. The color is black, like the clouds, like the soot ones, the demons of this world. Slave ants. Pain level is eight; my skin is crawling.

"Let me fix that; you need to concentrate."

Pain level is between a four and five; it's teetering but tolerable.

"Thank you," I say.

"It's a necessary fix." The Scarred One says, "When the time is right, the pain will kick in again. That's when you channel it."

"I don't like this." I take a turn to go deeper into the city. "How do we know we'll find the Dead One's new hideout, and the entrance to Death Highway?"

"When the time comes, we'll know."

"Dually noted." I say.

What was once a flourishing area for people to catch concerts, Broadway shows, and a few loved pubs is gone now. What was once the center of Providence has morphed into the city of The Dead One. These areas are where the Red Plane and our world now coexist.

On this two-lane street, we had no choice but to drive in a single file. On both sides, sidewalks and most of the street, decimated cars that look like something large had stepped on them litter the streets. There's only enough room for us to weave in and out. We coast our vehicles instead of blindly driving fast into unknown territory. Everything is so alien, constantly reshaping itself, shifting and contorting until the buildings are done, and the ant like creatures move on to the next objective.

Something bumps off my windshield, startling me. It falls from my view before I can see what it is, but it left a splatter of red on the passenger side of the windshield. The blood drips down in rivulets.

"What the hell?"

Another thump; this one bounces off the hood of my car. Then another. I see the severed stump, the mess of hair, rolled up eyes and tongue sticking out of the upturned mouth. Heads. It's raining heads.

"The residence of this section are throwing them at you." The Scarred One says.

"Randy!" Jack calls over the radio, "Are you seeing this shit?"

"Yes."

"Hey, Jack!" Alex speaks, "Thanks for the heads up!"

"There's something wrong with him."

"You're telling me." I look around; the residents that The Scarred One's talking about are ape like, with bald heads, and long arms that reach the floor. Their jaws hang low, the length of their chest, and they have a mouth full of endless teeth.

They don't stop. The heads rain down like hail.

"Don't they ever run out of ammo!" Will's voice yells over the radio.

"Cut to the right, we are in the slums of their world." The Scarred One says, "We'll encounter more, but, hopefully, we can get a little more speed instead of being slow moving targets."

I did as the Scarred One suggested; I cut to the left onto the next street. The buildings look the same as the others, run down, windowless and heavily charred, not the hint of black onyx like the taller buildings. I am starting to think this world was a place for the rich and the poor, as well. A viscous cycle throughout all the universes.

More of the ape like creatures appear in their windows, using their long arms to throw more decapitated heads. I can speed up to evade most attacks, a head here or their thumps against my passenger door. That's going to leave a mark, bastards.

One of them, much taller than the ones throwing heads, comes out from the gaping doorway of one of the buildings to my left, charging towards my car, using his arms to thrust him forward faster than a normal ape would in our world. I brace for impact.

The hear the sound of a shotgun; the spray takes off half its face stopping it dead in its tracks. Others follow what their fellow ape creature tried to do. They are charging in groups now. My window is down, left hand out, firing the snub nose. I take down four with head shots, one with two to the chest. Behind me, the others have opened fire as well, leaving a litter of bodies in their wake. They keep coming; the numbers grow as everyone is reloading.

The Scarred One waves my right hand in a motion like throwing a frisbee at the large group charging us. Their heads twist around, necks snap instantly, and the bodies drop dead. Others retreat into the shadows once they watched the others die from an invisible force. I cut hard to the right. The buildings are changing from slums to newer areas, a combination of our old Providence and the New Providence.

The road opens to recreational areas, which are pretty much fissure laden grounds with surging lava peeking through the cracks. Construction sites where the foundations of the buildings are concreted flesh, it's writhing and moaning. The beams that make up the buildings are elongated bones that belong to giants instead of the usual humans.

Ahead, a shimmering wall stretches across the horizon. Behind it, coming into view, is a steel building with three smoke stacks sticking from its roof. Ashen grey smoke rises out of the stacks. It blinks in and out of existence. If I keep my eyes still, the building is solid.

It's the Dead One's lair, the final one to hold the race to Death Highway. This is it.

All we must do to get there is drive through hundreds of suicidal cultists.

13.

It almost seemed it would work. The bodies bounce off our cars as we run down the fanatics. The sound of them, when hit, makes me shudder. Their skin is black like soot. I notice the crazed symbols carved into their bodies; they are red and raw. Their bodies are made of nothing when we hit them. They nearly explode on impact. My windshield wiper blades wipe away the blood. It takes forever; they keep coming.

"This is pointless."

Midnight Beauty rocks back and forth. The ones that don't die are getting impatient and angry. They start attacking the car. I barely see the others in my rearview mirror, numerous cultists block my view.

"This is getting us nowhere," I say.

We decided to stay single file again; it seemed an easier way to keep an eye on each other. But I can't tell what is safe for us.

"Let me try. There are a lot of them., I don't know if I can hold them off for too long but maybe just long enough to get through."

Just like earlier with the ape creatures, the Scarred One flicks his wrist, a bunch of the soot cultists separate, like he is parting the red sea. Some fall back in with the larger crowd; other bodies can't handle the strength of the invisible force and explode the moment The Scarred One unleashes the power. We now have a clear road. I can feel him straining against the bodies as they pile up on each other to fight the invisible force field.

"Go now!"

I shift gears; Midnight Beauty leaps forward. I press on the gas, and I hear the others rev up their cars. They are right behind me as I speed through the path the Scarred One has created for us. He's sweating, which makes me sweat. My eyes are blurry with fatigue. The few that escape meet my front bumper; my car thumps as I run over another. The same is happening with the crew; here and there a cultist breaks the hold and kills itself by running into their cars.

Gunfire erupts, coming from Alex's car. The Scarred One is getting weaker.

"Come on, hold on longer," I say, gritting my teeth. I try to focus my mind, maybe help give him some strength. I had to break the hold when a blackened fist smashes my driver side window. I fire shots into his chest, shattering the window as well. I close my eyes; some glass cuts my face. They are reaching for me through the window. I grab the small axe I keep on my seat, just in case, and hack away at their hands. They don't pull back. They try to attack with their bloody stumps.

"I got another idea," The scarred one says. I feel his mind, the right side of my brain, shift. The shield completely weakens. They rush in; bodies collide with metal, denting the doors. They fall over from purposely smashing their heads. Others run over the falling, stomping them as they go.

I hear the ground erupt to the right, where the fissures are. Scarred One splits the ground open even more; lava spills out, a river of it slowly heads our way. The cultists cheer, a large portion of them run towards the hot liquid. They scream in joy as they jump into it, obliterating their bodies.

Our cars shake back and forth as the mob runs by the cars. Some jump over, their feet padding my roof. I clench my jaw as they dent the hood.

"Some are still remaining."

They are in front of the Dead One's lair. Now that we are closer, the gray ash coming out of the stacks looks like screaming faces. I charge the car into the small group of cultists who have no interest in the lava bath.

I run the car into the group in front, stopping me short. Their bodies are trapped under the car as I keep pressing the accelerator; the tires burn into their bodies. Screw this. I get out of the car, hatchet in hand and start chopping through the remaining ones, piece by piece.

Laura is beside me, blasting gun fire into the faces of the ones nearby, fighting off others in close combat with a machete blade. Then Alex, Will, and Jack are in the mix. More gun fire, body parts embracing blade, their blood burns when it hits me. I don't care; nothing is stopping me, stopping us.

There is nothing left to kill. The screams in the air are followed by sizzling flesh. There's a trail of bodies in our wake. The Scarred One moves them with our mind, pushing the bodies aside and out of the path to clear the way for good this time.

We are all breathing heavy, battle lust in our faces. We don't need to say anything; it's done. It's time. We get in our cars and drive toward the warehouse to face the Dead One.

We race through the industrial area. It may be different from all the others, different buildings and layout of the area. But where we are going, the meeting place will always be the same. Even if we don't know where to go, the world is ever shifting; it will lead us to our destination.

The entrance to the Warehouse is a gaping mouth; we drive into the darkness. The area is huge. Stairs along all sides of the building lead up to walkways above our heads. There's another garage door up ahead. We stop our cars and get out. This is the farthest we can go.

The place fills with dark figures, followers of The Dead One. On the stairs, the walkway, they fill the space around us. Their maddening whispers fill the large space like the droning of bees. It's almost in my head. I can see it bothering the others. Eyes of fire appear in the darkness ahead. I am prepared to see the true form of the Dead One, not of the human we dealt with years ago. Instead, the owner of those eyes steps out. His face is fissured like the wasteland we had driven through. The cracks light up with the lava surging through him. He's wearing a leather jacket that looks super imposed onto his fiery body. His beer belly sticks out like a molten rock. In his hand, there is a long chain with a hook that's on fire.

"Come on, Randy. Want to go a few rounds? For old time sakes."

Cody. My heart drops. His face appears in my mind again, the look of helplessness as I tried to save him.

"I don't like him," The Scarred One says, "I know I did bad things to you out of desperation, but your friend here, he's a different type of evil. He loves it here. You shouldn't feel bad for someone who burns for destruction."

"You're right," I say.

Cody swings his chain, faster and faster. I told the others to stand back. The dark figures' whispering is faster. I clench my right hand, preparing for the attack.

"STOP!"

The place trembles. A figure, standing over seven feet tall, steps out of the shadows. His chiseled body is shirtless; it's covered with the faces of the damned; they moan in torment. He's still wearing jeans. They are ripped; the holes showing the slick flesh underneath. He's almost done with his transformation with this world. A tusk curls out from his forehead, bends back almost to the back of his head. His beady eyes are a dead yellow; his jaw is long when it opens, taking form like the other beings. His tattoos are sizzling. Laura grabs my arm in fear; she's trembling.

"Are you here for Death Highway?" he asks in a booming voice.

I step forward. "You know we are."

He nods. We wait for what he's going to say next.

"Then Death Highway you will race."

The dark figures whisper in excitement.

"Race rules," The Dead One continues, "Elimination circuit."

Every being in the building goes nuts, talking amongst themselves in a fast speech. They are placing their bets. Here we go.

"Only one can cross Death Highway. Only one." He says this with determination in his voice. "Stipulation. Gauntlet rules. There will be others you have to battle that will try and stop you. It's a free for all."

Collective gasps.

"Do you accept?"

I look to my crew. It was inevitable. They knew it, we all knew it. Something like this would happen. Laura's fingers cross with mine as she holds my hand. Will nods to me, then Alex, and Jack.

"Yes," I say, "We accept."

PART THREE
DEATH HIGHWAY

14.

There it is. I am finally here. We are finally here. Death Highway. I've waited so long, gone through hell and back to face this legend, to drive down it's eternal asphalt to find a means to an end for all of this. For me. For us. Cars idle with bated breath, waiting for the go ahead. I grip my steering wheel, knuckles popping with anxiety. I wipe my sweaty hands on my jeans, not wanting them to slip off the steering wheel at the wrong moment.

The red sky is alive with a light show, lighting the color of veins scatters across the horizon. There are cracks in the sky. They spread across like a damaged sheet of glass about to collapse at any moment. The weight of the Universe is getting heavier. The mountains seem to close in slowly like glaciers. Most of the land at the starting point is the barren waste of nuclear sand. I can't even begin to imagine what gauntlet of inhabitants and forces of nature we'll have to face here.

Our cars are lined up at the starting line in this order: I'm in front, Cody's car to my right, Laura behind me, and Jack's car is next to her. In the rear, Alex and Will.

"Hey, Will," Alex's voice speaks over the radio.

"Yeah?"

"We're in the rear."

"Ha! Good one."

Their laughter fills my car. It eases my already tense shoulders, and the tightness in my neck. I can't help but smile. The crew is together again. Even if Cody is a murdering monster made of burning cinders, it wouldn't feel complete without him here at the starting line, right up front with me. It's always been the two of us in the lead. The good old days, kind of. I'm aware that it might have to come down to killing my friends, and the love of my life, to cross the finish line. Maybe it will be my life that ends instead and one of them will win; it's a worthy sacrifice if one of them can change things for the better. If it comes to that, I'm ok with it; I've made my peace.

"I'm going to end you, Jones," Cody's voice, guttural and raw threatens over the radio.

I've had enough battle of words. I respond with the revving of Midnight Beauty's engine and flash him a shit eating grin. He responds back by accelerating his Pontiac GTO, a fire breathing dragon. The engine block sticking out of the hood proves that when the flames burst from the pipes. His entire car is fire, the small bluish flames lap on the surface.

The dark figures cheer, unable to contain their excitement any longer. The loud speakers crackle, a charismatic voice bellows from them, getting the crowd even more riled up. Their feet pummel the ground, the stairs and the overhead walkways. Their hands slap crazily on the railings, a chaotic tribal percussion mixed with chants and screaming. The energy is electric and terrifying. Alex, Will, and even Jack are revving their engines, keeping the momentum going.

I look in the rearview mirror at Laura behind me; our eyes lock. We hold each other in our gazes. I can see the nervousness in her face, but she's like the rest of us; once this thing starts, we will become very different people. We are competitive and, yes, even a little blood thirsty.

Seconds bleed out; the anticipation is building.

The horn wails. Immediately following its cry, the roar of the crowd is muffled by the union of screeching tires all going at the same time. For a second, I couldn't see anyone behind me because of all the smoke. My car shoots forward onto Death Highway, Cody's right next to me, going neck and neck. The others aren't too far behind. How do we go about this? Should I start shooting at them first? No, I'm not ready for it to come down to that. If there are others about to join the party, then it's best to let things play out from there. Opportunity provides entry.

Besides, I still have Cody to deal with.

As if on cue, just as he crosses my thoughts, he swipes his car into mine. The flames roll off and transfer onto my car; they go out quickly. He's playing. He's testing the waters to determine which one of us is capable of what. I'll bite. I cut the wheel hard in his direction; our cars collide. He loses control and veers off the road and onto the ashen sand. The sand kicks up in clouds as he regains his control; the intense horsepower of his vehicle allows him to quickly catch up.

"You're quiet."

"Yes." The Scarred One replies.

"What's up with that?"

"Waiting. And enjoying the scenery. I am going to miss this place."

I don't say anything. I can feel his sorrow; he can feel my regret. But we both have an understanding; there's no other choice.

We come up to a sign that reads: HUNTING GROUND

"What's the hunting ground?"

"More hogs, and the things that poach them."
As the Scarred One says that, the herd seems to come out of nowhere as they run alongside the road, but not going into it. They stay on the sand, legs pumping fast, keeping up with our vehicles.

In the distance, other vehicles make their way across the land, heading towards the herd. The mutant hogs sense danger; they are so frightened that they enter the road, trying squeeze in with our cars. They grow agitated and fearful. They start attacking the cars, throwing their many tusked heads from side to side, trying to swipe the cars. One managed to connect with Alex's car, hitting the left fender; he swerves, brakes, and then regains control.

"I hate these things!" Alex's window rolls down, his arms sticks out, automatic gunfire erupts taking out the hog that attacked him. He continues to shoot any of them within range. Will joins the fight, shots blast from the hand gun he is wielding.

I'm about to pump bullets into the hog that's pursuing me when one of the other vehicles pulls up. A net shoots out from a device attached to the back of the pickup truck and scoops up the animal. It squeals as whatever the material the net is made from singes and cuts into the flesh. It smells of bad meat being cured. The device drops the trapped animal; it lands hard in the cab. The captor peers at me; its head is small with two beady black eyes, and no mouth. It's head splits apart sideways revealing its mouth; it screeches into the sky.

"What's it pissed about? Because I'm messing with its food or because we are on Death Highway?

"Both." The Scarred One replies.

"That's great." I swerve into the monster truck, a desperate attempt to run the vehicle into the rock lodged in the sand. It easily jumps off it like the rock is a ramp. It lands, the suspension squeaks, and the truck returns to its position at my side.

It's too late when I notice the device that harnessed the net is now loaded with a harpoon. I move quickly, shifting gears to gain speed. The harpoon gun fires; the point lodges into the body of my car just past the door. That could've been me.

The truck pulls, trying to bring my car into the desert with it. I cut the wheel the other direction. While we are having our tug of war, more gunfire. Laura is fighting off another monster truck of these creatures. She had opened fire on them the moment they got close to her. The windshield of that truck is splattered with green blood as the bullets riddle the driver's body. The truck cuts hard and tips over; the creature in the back flies and does a somersault on the asphalt only to get hit by the purple Cuda. It lays, unmoving, off the side of the road.

The creature in the pickup that's attached to Midnight Beauty screeches in anger, and throws his scaly arms in the air, frustrated. He begins climbing down the metal wire, closing the distance between our vehicles quickly. He reaches for my steering wheel. I cut it toward the truck, catching the driver off guard, and slamming the reptilian being into the truck, crushing its body between both vehicles. It doesn't shake him off. Using my right hand, I grab the snub nose and empty all six bullets into its mouth, or head, or whatever it is before it clamps on my face. It loses its grip and falls beneath my wheels. There's the sound of twisting metal. The harpoon gun comes loose; the stand and the base pull from the cab. The momentum releases the truck with such force the driver does not have time to jump the next rock rushing towards it. The vehicle flips over and explodes in a fireball of smoke.

There's not enough time to warn the others about the large piece of equipment trailing behind me, being pulled by the harpoon that is still attached to my car. I try to retain control as it bounces around from side to side, shifting the car with it. I only hope whoever is behind me has seen the whole thing take place and is wise to keep a safe distance.

"Allow me."

The scars writhe and squirm as The Scarred One calls upon the power. Not much, not wanting to exert himself, just enough for what he needs to do. The harpoon wiggles and then pulls free. The harpoon gun and its station bounce once on the asphalt. The Scarred One moves it toward the few hogs that are left and takes them out. They go down like bowling balls, and then the harpoon stand slams the remaining trucks. The imaginary hand lunges the harpoon into the driver. The truck flips over, taking out the two drivers behind it.

Cody scorches one near him; the flames jump from his car and cover the truck. The creatures are screeching; the sound cuts off when the vehicle finally explodes.

"There ya go," he says over the radio, "I contributed to the team."

Alex, Will, and Laura leave a trail behind them of smoldering trucks and bullet riddled mutant hogs. Most of the creatures have been killed or have moved on. The same with the drivers. They end their pursuit of the beasts and of them, as well.

"Funny," I say. "They looked like they were spooked by something."

"We are entering territory they want no part of; the thing that rides here is a vile creature. He is known as The Collector."

15.

The area we drive through next is a desolated town. It's look like something from picturesque America 1950's got hit by the atomic bomb. Instead of driving through neighborhoods, it's as if parts of that time got blown separately from each other and landed in the Red Plane in random sections along Death Highway.

The first thing I saw was a rustic gas station, with the old gas pumps. The sands of time have covered half of the structure. Every house used to have the look like it was pulled out of a postcard. But, like the gas station, every dream is weather beaten, stripped down and decimated by the conditions of this world.

The sense of dread that the reptilian creatures felt is very much present in this part of Death Highway. There is a malevolent force lurking close by. The reptilians and the hogs might just be frightened creatures who don't like intruders in their area and react the way they do once threatened. I don't blame them.

Whatever is here thrives on chaos and madness.

A building looms tall up ahead. It's made of the similar black onyx stone the creatures used to build their city and for New Providence. Upon closer look, it appears to be a station. Only one set of train tracks lead out from it, going the opposite direction, east along the desert. There isn't a sign of any trains leaving, no bustling about of people waiting to take any form of transportation from this strange station. It's just here, smack dab in the middle of a desert, along an eternal highway. The statue in front of the building is one of a ghoulish looking thing, dressed in a bus driver uniform. He's even got a transportation driver's cap on his head. I don't think I have ever seen anyone wear those anymore. I couldn't wait to get out from under the shadow of this building and that statue. Of all the things I've witnessed, this one really fills me with dread.

There's a tunnel attached to the building; however, there's no road that leads to it. To get to the tunnel, one would have to drive off road and onto the sand. There's no doubt that tunnel leads to the station. A sound comes from the tunnel; whatever it is, it's moving fast. A bull horn blares from within. The tunnel is a mouth and it bellows the noise like a creature of immense size.

"What the hell is that?" Jack asks.

"Whatever it is, it's big," Alex says.

"Randy? Anything from our mutual friend?"

I sigh, "The Scarred One calls it The Collector."

"What the hell does that mean?" Will asks.

We are about the find out.

The thing making the gigantic noise speeds out of the tunnel like a bullet; its huge wheels cuts through the sand with no problem. The vehicle is slightly bigger than the ones we were used to back home. Something about its metallic surface shines more than it should, organic and flesh like.

"What the hell? A bus?" Jack asks.

"Guys be careful of that thing," I warn," You don't know what it's capable of." But then again, neither do I.

"Do you know what to expect Scarred One?"

I can feel him shaking my head. "He collects damned souls that have nowhere to go. Some easily go with him; some must be influenced, lied to, or just completely tricked. If he's on Death Highway, then he's got a good reason. There's nothing random about this being."

The bus rolls up in the lane next to me. Cody sees this as opportunity and speeds up. He's going to move in when the time is right for him, and that makes him one of the most dangerous in this race.

The driver is the ghoulish figure represented by the statue back at the station. His skin is the color of bluish mold. The skin is worn so thin it looks like a skull under that bus cap and spots cover his face like crypt moss. He leers at me with white eyes; no pupils can be seen. His mouth forms a lipless grin.

He grabs the radio speaker from above. "Ladies and gentlemen, ladies and gentlemen!" The people riding the bus turn to look at the driver. The lighting inside of the bus is tinted a dirty green. When it flickers, it reveals the decimated souls underneath the people riding this terrible thing.

His finger points accusingly at me. "You see this piece of monkey shit driving next to us?"

They all turn their collective heads in my direction at once.

"This one here and his merry band of assholes are here to destroy what you worked hard for, what you earned in this world that is rightfully yours. Well, they are here to take it all away, all for themselves. Let's show the greedy bastards how we welcome their treachery in our world!"

The lights flicker. They go from lost shambles of a human soul to something more sinister, something corrupted by the poison of this thing's tongue and its cursed vehicle. Their bodies contort and stretch upward; their flesh is black and shiny with scales. They have no eyes; their mouths open, hanging low as they hiss.

All the bus windows drop open.

The opening looks too small for the demonic beings to be able to fit through. Somehow, they manage to contort their bodies and push through the opening. First the head, gelatin like, pushes out, and then the long arms. The creature places its hands on the outside of the bus and pushes, slipping the rest out with ease. Others follow, doing the same with their bodies. Now there's three or four of them crawling around the bus like fish riding a whale, eating the bacteria off its body.

The first one lifts its head towards me and hisses. It leaps from the bus; the strength of the thing forces the large vehicle to lean to one side. In one jump, from the bus to the asphalt, it closes the distance to my car. Midnight Beauty nearly loses control when it lands sideways, attaching itself to the passenger side of my car. I regain control of my car. The creature scurries to the front of the car, standing on the hood, blocking my view. It's head cocks to one side then the other; I stare right back. The Scarred One is reloading the cylinder of the snub nose. I want to admire the trick he's managing of doing it all one handed while I drive, but I'm afraid, if I take my eyes off my assailant, I could pay a heavy price. It moves quickly on all fours, making its way to my window. The Scarred One passes the hand gun to me with my right hand and then takes the wheel, keeping the car steady, while I pump some bullets into the ugly bastard.

The first shot misses. The creature moves with lighting quick reflexes. I miss again, but then the side of its head explodes when the other three hit their target. I stare into the abyss; it too bleeds black. The creature tries to shake off the damage to take a swipe at me, but quickly grows weak and loses its grip on my car door. My back tire thumps as I run over its body.

Laura is getting attacked, having a difficult time shaking it off. The Scarred One uses my right hand to down shift, as I brake to line up with Laura's car. I pass the gun over to my right side, so I can take the wheel, steadying the car as we back up with one side of the car on sand and the other on asphalt. The gun is reloaded and passed to me. I shift gears as we come around the rear of Laura's car. My arm sticks out, and I start firing at the creature on the passenger side of the purple Cuda. It's body jerks as the bullets strikes it. It loses its grip, and thump, another one under my tires. Wish I was keeping score.

Laura and I move forward so Alex and Will are now aligned with the bus on the left side of it. Jack maneuvers himself so he's driving on the sand, coming up to the right side of the bus where other shadow creatures wait to be unleashed. He starts firing. The blackened bodies jerk, like they are dancing, as the bullets rip through them. Alex and Will empty rapid fire bullets into the two beings still latching onto the bus. The bus shudders as it takes the damage; the two creatures are dead on the asphalt.

"Hey, Randy." Alex calls over the radio.

I grab the speaker. "Yeah, what's up."

"Dude, the bus is bleeding. I'm not shitting you. We swiss cheesed it, taking out the last two of those things; red shit is dripping from the holes."

I hang up the speaker; the radio squawks.

"You assholes are in a whole lot of hurt now," The Collector says.

I snake my car between Laura and the bus, speeding up. Once I got enough distance, I cut the wheel, downshift, and do a one eighty so that I am facing the front of the bus and I keep the car in reverse.

"Randy," Laura says, "This is not the time to get fancy, babe."

The Scarred One and I do our trick of switching hands from the wheel to reloading the gun, and then he takes the wheel again while the .38 is in my left hand, hanging out the window. I fire off shots at the bus. Three holes appear in the window to the right of the driver. The next two hit their mark. Black blood splatters the windshield, obscuring his view. The bus swerves left and then right. He's losing control. The body of the bus squirms as it rights itself back in the lane.

"Did you see that?" I ask.

"Yes." The Scarred answers.

There's a horrible screeching sound of metal on metal as the bus tears itself apart. The top half pulls away from the bottom. The middle of the grill is now an open mouth, the torn shards are teeth. Inside the mouth is a churning abyss of gears and machinery, all meant to break down flesh and bone of the unfortunate souls to be consumed by this nightmarish creature.

"Oh yeah!" The Collector yells excitedly over the radio, "How do you like her now!"

The bus monster roars in response. Its mouth opens wider. It's gaining speed, about to close the gap between us. We need to think of something or we'll be the ones ground up in the organic machinery.

"I got this!" Will yells over the radio.

His car speeds up, fits in between my car and the monster bus just right. The mouth is close to Will's car now; the bottom teeth scrapes against the bumper.

"Will! What are you doing?"

"What needs to be done my brother, I don't just build land mines in the woods." He smiles at me.

Oh, shit. He rigged his NOS tank.

"You might want to get out of the way."

The back of Will's car is fully inside the mouth of the bus. It chomps down, metal crunching and grinding on metal. The bus feeds on Will's car, up to the rearview mirror now. The front wheels spark and burn; the front of Will's bumper skids on asphalt.

"Makaveli Mother Fucker!"

I cut the wheel and drive onto the sand, pulling away from the bus just in time. Will's car explodes. It makes a fiery crater in the things mouth. The monster grill catches fire, smoke obscures the windows. The creature squeals in pain. It loses control. It shifts to the right, then to the left, nearly clipping Alex and Jack, then back to the right and off Death Highway.

At this point, I've performed another one eighty turn, car facing forward. I'm back on the road, watching the bus creature. It's writhing back and forth trying to get rid of the fire. The bus flips over, insectile legs grow out from the bottom. It wiggles like a pill bug stuck on its back. It was mewling in pain, kicking up sand everywhere.

"This isn't over," The Collector says, "I'm not easily killed; I'll find you."

I leave no reply.

We move onward. We've caught up with Cody. He smiles at me; I give him the finger. I want to ask him if he enjoyed the show, watching our friend give his life like that. But, then again, I remind myself that those are the rules The Dead One set.

"Will, man, I can't believe it," Alex says over the radio.

"I know," I answer.

I can hear that Alex is getting choked up. Then he asks, "Were his last words a Tupac quote?"

I smile. "Yep."

"That fucking,"- he busts out laughing. I don't hear Laura or Jack over the radio, but I can see their smiles in the mirror.

"Can we just kill each other and get this shit over with?" Alex asks.

"I'm ok with that," Cody adds.

Up above, a black cloud is heading towards us; it's faster than the others. It breaks apart in swarms.

16.

    The swarm swoops down. They vary in size, from that of a small dog to a full human.
    It's all I see, these alien insects, flooding my vision. I keep driving. The smaller ones hit the windshield, busting open. Green shit that's supposed to be blood drips down the windshield on the passenger side. I'm still able to turn the wheel and shift out of the way when the bigger one's charge at me, though it's hard to see amongst the countless swarm.
    I hear gunfire, but I can't tell who's shooting. The only one I can see is Cody's car. The flames grow in height. The bugs crash into them and burn. Some die and roll off his hood a smoldering corpse; others fly away engulfed in flames.
    One of the bigger ones catches me off guard when I swerve to avoid one that's a similar size. It crashes through the middle of my windshield. It buzzes madly as it tries to break free. I can still see, so I continue to focus on the driving, but I need to do something about this thing. If it destroys the rest of my windshield, I am screwed. I picture my body overrun by these things; my body shivers.
    Getting a good look at this thing, I see that it has spikes that run across its back. The wings are more

mammal, a dark purple with yellow veins running through the flaps of the wings. The head looks like it would belong to a worm, just a little larger and rounder. It opens, a long mouth snaps out trying to attack.

"Oh shit!" I grab the snub nose and fire all six bullets into its mouth and round head. It's dying but not completely dead yet. It's still advancing on me.

"Fuck this."

The Scarred One grabs it by the extra mouth and rips it out. The bright shit green blood drips from the wound and the severed piece. He throws it to the floor, then grabs under the round head and squeezes, I almost gag at the smell of it as it oozes over my hand. It goes into death throes before it finally dies, still in my windshield.

"At least it can't do any more damage." The Scarred One says.

I don't argue. He reloads the .38. Now what. This swarm seems like it could last the rest of the ride on Death Highway. My car rocks back and forth some more from the impact of the bugs. I can hear new dents getting created with each larger one that strikes the side of my car.

"We need to do something. I don't know how much damage any of our cars can take."

"I'm going to borrow some fire."

I see a huge flame light up nearby. The things squeal in pain as they burn. It's Cody's car; the Scarred One is now controlling his flames. With the flick of the wrist, streams of it like a blow torch lights up the swarm. Laura's car is nearby. Some of the things are latched on to the Cuda; they burn to a crisp and fall.

"Where's Alex? And Jack?"

Scarred One lights up another area. I can see Jack's car, as the ones that latched onto it have died now.

"Dude," Alex calls, "I think I'm done for."

I grab the radio. "Where are you, hang on, we got a way out."

"I think I got pushed back too far, half my windshield is smashed." I can hear them now, buzzing crazily. Alex screams, something tears.

"Alex!"

"I'll see you around, buddy. I am piggy backing on Will's heroic exit. Peace!"

Somewhere behind us, we hear an explosion. Alex must have popped a couple of grenades and let them sit on top of the NOS tanks. The swarm finally clears. Death Highway and the Red Plane never looked so good, after having a swarm of angry cosmic bugs in your face.

"Can we get rid of that please?" I ask, pointing to the carcass of the thing. My right hand opens; the force of air pushes it out. It lands in the road and then meets my tires.

"How bad is everyone's damage?" I ask.

Sounds like whoever's left, Laura, Jack, and myself have suffered the same dents in our cars. Their windshields have some cracks, but nothing close to the gaping hole in mine.

"I'm doing great," Cody chimes in. I ignore him. If it's just me and him in the end, I swear I'm the one who's going to end him.

"Can we fix any of the damage?"

"I should really save my energy, Randy, I have a feeling what's coming next will make The Collector look like kid stuff. "

"Shit. What could be worse than that lunatic?"

"The Death Stalkers." The Scarred One replies.

Why did I ask?

17.

Things are coming out of the sand. We've driven maybe ten miles. I don't know about everyone else but I am thankful for the break. The only thing that kept me tense was Cody. He hasn't really tried anything since the start of the race. Since we met the onslaught of residents of Death Highway, he's been spectating. I expect him to strike at any moment. Right now, I am thankful for the quiet. I am just trying to enjoy the drive, even if it's a landscape that'll kill you.

I first noticed there were things coming out of the sand when I saw the way the ground moved. I took it for a mound at first, the size expanding a trick of the heat mirage. Then the mound got larger, and the sand pulled away.

Engines shriek, the sound is horrifying, piercing my ears.

"You see these things," Jack asks.

"Yeah," I answer.

" Just be ready," Scarred One says, " These may be the Deathstalkers. Apparently they are worse than the bus monster."

"What? How's that even possible?"

I look in my rearview mirror at one of the nearly risen creatures, but I don't know what I am looking it. It looks like a mound of flesh with two wheels.

"Randy!"

I look up in time to see one heading in my direction, and fast too. I swerve just in time to get out of its way. My car rocks from the sheer force of its speed. In the rearview mirror, I see it turn sideways, barely slowing down. It is easily able to maneuver on two wheels, even at that speed. I had lost count since the first mound; what was that ten? Twenty of them? If that's the case, we are outnumbered, and they are closing in fast. The open air is surrounded by their engines, loud and powerful enough to make your ears bleed.

The one that nearly had a head on collision with me catches up and drives up to my driver's side. I see its colors, a beautiful glow of blues and greens all over its pulsating body. I can't see where any evidence of a bike would be. Where the exhaust pipes would normally be located are four writhing appendages. They move like impatient fingers thrumming. It's head peels from the front; the top of its body pulls away with slime trailing. The long appendage is segmented with an oval-shaped tip. It peels back to reveal a very big stinger.

"Oh fuck!" I swerve away from it just before it swung that tail at me, the tip of the stinger just barely scraping my car. A claw peels from the mechanism its attached to; it opens and closes as if taunting me. The thing closes in and unleashes a combo attack, claw, tail, claw. Before it can go for another attack, Scarred One gives me the gun and he takes the wheel. The creature shrieks in anger as I fire bullets into its side. Its head looks at me, no eyes, the mandibles twitch angrily. It backs away.

"A scorpion! The Deathstalkers are scorpions on wheels!"

Yeah. Don't you have Deathstalkers in your world?

"Yes! But not scorpion biker gangs that are fused to their vehicles! What the hell are they?"

"At one time, from ancient Sumeria, the Scorpion people were guardians. Now they are guardians of Death Highway."

"Great! Just fucking great!" I grab the speaker to the CB radio. "Poisonous?"

"Very!" The Scarred One says.

"You're a great guide, you know that? Hey Laura, Jack. Watch for those things; they are scorpions, and very poisonous."

"What!" Jack says.

"Is that what it transformed to when it attacked you?" Laura asks.

I watch both sides of the road, the others are closing in fast.

"Yeah, I'm getting the way things are here. The poison could eat your car; don't let that shit happen."

Within moments, we were opening fire. I had to make my shots extremely accurate. I am running out of bullets, and it takes nearly the whole cylinder or more to make them fall. Once they do, they are pretty much down. So, I take careful aim, tread water by letting them get close enough to be able to strike with their tail. I fire, the head explodes. The tires stop short and it flips over; its body lays on the ground dead. I look a little longer in my mirror; the freaking thing was huge with its body unfurled like that.

"We have grenades." The Scarred One says.

"Well, let's light shit up."

Scarred One reaches into the bag behind the seat and pulls out two grenades, holding them in our hand. A biker closes in, the sound of metal getting struck by its' tail. I speed up to put some distance between us. I hear the acid sizzling, the metal bubbling. I can smell liquid metal. Scarred One pops the pins and throws them out the passenger window. They float in the air for a couple seconds, then he directs them to the two nearest bikers. The grenades explode, and the creatures crash to the ground. Pieces of blue green flesh and machinery scatter around their corpses.

Laura has been doing well. I'm impressed with how many she's been taking out. I worry about how many bullets her automatic weapons have left. We've all been battling for a while, and it's not like we have been able to scavenge our dead friends' things to restock our inventory.

More mounds grow out of the sands. We are in serious trouble. My eyes go wide. I reach for the radio to warn Jack, but it's too late. One of the Deathstalkers, going insane speeds, gains on his car in no time. By the time I could even reach the radio, it had leapt in the air. The wheels suck into its torso, freeing its eight legs. It lands on top of Jack's car and rips off the roof like a can opener.

I speed up. The Scarred One is aiming my gun at it. He fires; the bullet strikes it, but doesn't slow it down. The legs pin Jack down, the claws are tearing at his flesh. He's screaming, but the look on his face is that of a warrior who won't go down.

"Go Randy! This isn't the end, this is only the beginning!" His Uzi is in his hand; he's got it up against the Deathstalker's stomach. He screams; the stomach lights up with bullets. He's lost in a hail of bullets, blood and torn flesh. The car loses control, goes off into the desert and flips over. Both Jack and the Deathstalker lay still.

Up ahead, the mountain is closing in. It's the same mountain I saw at the starting line. I now realize it's a massive organic mass. Two of them actually; they are moving toward each other, possibly to form new land, or new organisms. Either way, I do know that's the way through; the end is on the other side.

"Laura get in front of Cody, now! While he's distracted."

Cody is shooting off his flame thrower, out of his engine at the monster on top of his car, tearing into it. The Deathstalker is on fire, but that doesn't stop it. Another one comes up to his driver side. He reaches and grabs its head; it strikes his arm with its tail. The poison does nothing to his magma flesh, the tail burns off.

Laura gets in front, slows down and forces Cody to reduce speed. Many of the Deathstalkers continue their assault. They go after Laura. I fire my last bullets from the snub, getting perfect head shots. I swerve so I don't run over their fallen bodies.

We are almost at the moving mountains.

I move in to slam into Cody. I know my NOS is rigged, just from the look in Will's eyes when I last saw him. They had all been planning this, this suicide run. Even if we didn't like it, we knew that it was the only way to end the merging of the worlds.

"All of you were getting affected by the merge, other versions of you were dying but they were also molding into each other, as well." The Scarred One says, "The last version, all of you became killers to survive the underworld that street racing brought you into. You were all ready to die and kill each other because of that."

And I am ready to end myself.

"Go Laura, you got this. I'll stay behind; I'll take care of Cody."

I hear her screams over the radio..

"Laura?"

A dead scorpion nearly struck my car. I see the acid bubbling on her door; there's blood and flesh sticking to it, as well.

No! No!

"Laura!"

"Go Randy."

I can tell she's in pain.

"I'm done, the acid is moving fast," she cries out, hisses through her teeth, "It's you, it's always been you. End it, all for what we fought for. Go."

"Damn it!

Before I switch gears, I use my last three bullets, and fire them at Cody. The look of shock on his face is priceless, even better when it explodes into blood, bone and magma. He's not dead, but it's enough of a distraction, enough for Laura to keep him pinned.

I gun the engine. As I pass her, I see the damage. It's eaten most of her left shoulder; she's driving with one arm. The left is almost falling off. I look into her emerald green eyes one more time before bringing my car in front of her just in time.

On both ends, the organic mass is full of teeth and writhing things that may be tongues. They are close enough to lick my car. I shift gears again to push the speed past one hundred. Laura is slowing down significantly. Before the mass completely closes in on her, she slams on the brake, forcing Cody to rear end her. Then an explosion happens before they are swallowed up into nothing.

I am the last man standing.

I am the merger of all things.

I am the end.

I will not shed a tear.

There will be new worlds after this.

18.

This is not what I expect. After narrowly surviving the Deathstalkers and getting past that titanic mass of teeth, I did not expect to see this. I thought I'd be at the end. Instead, I am witnessing a surreal beauty of this world I didn't expect. The blood red tint to the sky is less over here; its faded like the colors of the sunset. I still don't see a sun, but there are stars in the inky blackness above. We are driving around the bend of a mountain. It amazes me that, during this whole journey, Midnight Beauty hasn't run out of gas.

A lake is below us. It's dark, the surface like black ice. Large worm-like creatures jump in and out of the dark water. They sound like whales. It's beautiful. There's a peaceful tranquility on this side of this world that I wouldn't even consider calling the Red Plane. Maybe this is what the end looks like here; this is the reward of surviving Death Highway. I understand why the wretched things want to protect it. It's the only thing that isn't touched by their madness, don't know if it will ever be, but they'll make sure it isn't for as long as they can.

Even the Scarred One is enjoying this; he hasn't said a word and I won't force him too either. I am surprised to find that I am sad our end is nearing, but it's better this way. At least I hope he thinks so, to end of all our pain and suffering.

"Yes. I agree. I am very tired." The Scarred One says.

"Me too, buddy. Me too."

We reach the top of the mountain. There's a long road the length of a drag racing strip. At the end of the road on the left is an open cave, on the right, The Dead One.

I rev my engine for what may feel like the final time.

"Choose," He says, his arm stretched out, pointing to the opening.

Choose what? I only see one entrance. Is this another one of his tricks?

The Dead One is in true form. He stands at nearly nine feet tall. He is completely naked, the crotch area smooth, no genitals of any type. His head, a long black tusk, seems longer than before. Maybe it's his height, but the black ivory head still curls behind to his thick neck. His chest is riddled with more tormented faces, all of them frozen in time. Great black wings stretch out from behind him, his shadow withers.

"Choose, Randy Jones, before it's too late."

"I don't understand."

"Randy look." The Scarred One says, "Behind him."

I see it. The rock surface is round, like the cave to my left, but it's closed off. The surface bares cracks; there's a light breaking from behind it. It pushes away the mass of his shadow. I shift the gears and stomp on the pedal.

"Here we go!"

The front lifts, the wheels screech. I will never get sick of the smoke, the tires burning into the ground below, the rush when it feels like I am flying as the car stays in the air. I press the switch for Tank One of the NOS tanks; she's off like a rocket, and we collide with The Dead One.

His huge body folds over the hood of the car. He's squealing; the sound of panic coming from him fills me with great joy and triumph. Out of all the things I have been wanting to defeat, even Death Highway itself, this is the true reward.

He scratches at my hood, tearing into the metal easily. She won't give; Midnight Beauty is still on her two back tires. Dead One's wings flap uselessly after they strike the mouth of the cave, the surface collapses when struck. We are driving through a small tunnel. The light is so close, it burns; the pain is beautiful and free. It's healing. The Dead One is on fire. His form melts into other organic masses. Eyes, and tentacles and mouths try to find purchase with my car, try to damage it. But they don't have any power. The earth slowly climbs back onto its axis. The cosmos stops spinning. Minds mend, souls shake off the soot that has corrupted their inner beings. Things are righting themselves. The Red stops bleeding; the wound is cauterized, healed with a burning hot poker that glows a bright white.

"You know what to do." The Scarred One says.

"You bet." My finger hovers over the button for Tank Two, Will's special delivery.

"It's been a pleasure, Randy Jones."

"Yes, it has, Scarred One."

The pain is intense as the scars squirm and begin pulling from my body.

I press the button.

My vision explodes.

EPILOGUE

The sun shines bright overhead in the clear blue sky. It is warm on my skin, warm like the smile on my face. This is how my life is supposed to be. We are on my porch now; Cody hands me a beer. Alex and Will grab a beer and four of us cheers. We went through hell and back but we made it, together.

Grandpa and Grandma arrive, moving slower up the porch steps now that they have gotten older. They too are still full of life, because life is what truly matters. My two-year old girl runs by me; her bright red curls bouncing. She squeals with excitement and runs right into Grandpa's arms. He cradles her in his arms and says hello to the Slaters as they are next to arrive.

John Slater shakes my Grandpa's hand, playfully gives his hand a squeeze to still see if the old man still has his strength. Jack walks up to me by the grill with a big cooler in his hands. He tells me the steaks are in the cooler, I tell him it's time to get those suckers on the grill.

The steaks are sizzling on the grill, the beers are flowing, and the hot summer air is just right with a kiss of a light breeze. Life floats on this breeze, full and vibrant as the trees in my yard. Perfection. And yet, I still feel sadness.

Everyone is here. Even Karen Blackwell, our secretary at the Auto Body shop stopped by to enjoy good food and good company. My smile betrays the overwhelming emptiness corroding my insides. There are two people in my life missing from this picturesque day, my mother and Laura.

When all of this started in the other reality, I was in prison and the ceiling above my bed was blank of any pictures. There was a good reason for that. Look what happened with Laura. I tried my best to not allow the Red Plane to use my mind to betray me, and still I had to face the nightmare my sins had caused. Laura had a miscarriage because of me, and the Red Plane turned our unborn baby into a creature of the abyss.

During the first convergence, when the wormhole had appeared in my garage and I barely escaped my bloodthirsty memories I saw my mother amongst them, staring at me from the window of my home while I was fighting off Chris's army of creatures. It still hurts when I think about her somber face, pale like the monsters of the Red Plane. After she had died years ago in an accident, I used to picture her smiling face as a glowing sun in my mind, until the Red Plane tainted it.

Even though I beat Death Highway and won, I still feel in some way I lost. I couldn't change the fact that my mother still died in the car with my alcoholic abusive father. I couldn't change the fact that I blamed myself because I wished for him to die and unfortunately, my mother died with him. My Grandparents adopted me and fought hard to give me a better life and the chance to grow up with a future. I learned how to fix cars from Grandpa, watching his every move. It helped keep my mind busy, and he added lifting weights as another means to help keep the anger at bay. Because no matter what, anger is always a stranger taking your hand; you need to stop before it becomes your friend.

Picked on many times, I learned how to fight under my Grandpa's training. The training helped greatly, and, day by day, year by year, I became more focused, more driven. Not wanting me to have to deal with the same kids I had fought in middle school and had to deal with their bullshit in freshman year, he had enrolled me into Votech classes to help further my interest in auto mechanics. During my years at this new school, I met the best of friends I could ever wish for. I graduated high school with a certificate in mechanics and a high school diploma. I went to college to better myself, just like Grandpa had asked of me. I still struggled sure; real life after high school wasn't meant to be easy.

I did my internship at Blackmore Auto Body and Repair. I worked with another high school buddy of mine Jack Slater and his dad, John Slater. I provided the skills I had learned from Grandpa, from school and applied them at the shop. I gained a name for myself; became one of the top young mechanics and was fortunate to work at one of the best auto body shops in Blackmore, Rhode Island.

Despite the success at my day job I still street raced at night. We were racing kings, just me and the boys. Our names carried on the wind between city buildings and on the roar of engines. We owned it; we were that good, and then I met Laura. She was a damn good racer as well and completed the crew. Sometimes days were tough at the shop, so I made extra money from the races. But the crew and I always knew it would end, especially after Chris died. Chris was our bookie, also a racer. He talked too much shit and challenged another racer. Chris lost control and struck the other car. His car became a fireball and both drivers died in the explosion. We swore to never step foot in underground racing ever again.

This is my true reality.

I look at my little girl smiling and laughing in my Grandpa's arms. Two years. My little girl is already two years old. She looks like her mother, and I could only imagine how much more she'll look like her as the years get lost on us. Two years since my wife passed giving birth. After we were done with the racing life, we learned Laura was with child. I asked her to marry me. We bought a house and made an amazing life together, short as it was, gone in a blink of an eye. I still see her on that day we met, getting out of her car after a race, taking off her helmet, shaking out her long red hair. It seems like forever. It seems like yesterday.

Now she's gone.

I won Death Highway to change it all. I've done everything right with a few speed bumps in the road, and still I lost her. I try to fight back tears every time I think of her. Not now. I can't cry now in front of everyone when we are having a great time.

This is the life I am meant to have, but I still see evidence of that other life. Cody has that look in his eyes, and for a fearful moment I think they will burst into flames and he would change back into the monster he was. With Alex, I see the thick veins pulsating in his neck and the white foam coming out of his mouth like he's suffering an overdose of heroin. Will, John and Jack are covered in their own blood from the multiple lacerations on their bodies. Grandma rubs at her chest as if she's about to suffer a heart attack, and Grandpa just has a far away stare. I can feel his mind slipping away. I won't dare look at what my two year old has become.

Me? I itch. I itch so bad I could scratch off my flesh and it'll still be there. Sometimes it feels like burns.

Other times it tingles. Sometimes there's nothing, for months, and then it comes out of nowhere. Lately, it's been more that usual. There's a shimmer dancing in front of my eyes. I tell myself it's from the heat coming off the grill. When I look at my family and friends they are back to normal again, laughing and enjoying each other's company.

After everyone leaves and says their goodbyes, I put my little girl to bed. Thankfully, the day had exhausted her and she was already asleep as I carry her up the stairs to her room. I stand over her as she peacefully sleeps in her crib, lightly snoring.

I listen to those soft sounds a few moments longer before I turn around. A fissure appears in the wall on the other side of my little girl's crib, a red light bleeds from the crack. I don't have the gift anymore, but when my mind collides with that other me, and I begin to itch, I feel the other. I feel the door. That's when I walk through it. I go to the Red Plane.

I walk across its desolated terrain, the ashen gray sand, and look upon mountains huge and writhing. The sky is bleeding red and plagued with infectious black clouds. I can see a city; it's far down the landscape, but it's there. It's a sinister version of the city of Providence.

Laura is sitting at the edge of a cliff; she's waiting for me. She's always waiting for me. Here I remember everything.

The pain from that other life hits me like a strong wind, not the breeze of the life I am living now, and, every time I come here, I wonder why I'd put myself through such unwanted pain. This wind is strong and relentless. The pungent smell of death rides this breeze, and lingers in my nose for too long.

But she's here. My love. My firecracker. My red haired beauty is alone in a red haze world. I sit beside her.

Every time I do, I am quiet. What can I say? So many things tumbling in my mind, like a car flipping over and over, the sound of twisted metal and shrieking. Forever tumbling. I can't seem to get my thoughts together. My right side itches.

"I miss you," I finally say. I think I say this every time.

"I know," she answers back, always surprising me. Her voice always sounds like her own. I fear there will be a day her voice won't belong to her, but to something else that lives in these forsaken lands. "I miss you, too. I am so alone here."

She looks just as I remember her. She's in her leather jacket and blue jeans. I can smell her perfume;

the sweet smell is powerful, over the smell of death of this place.

"This is the way I am meant to be," she says and smiles. Her eyes smile. But there's sadness there. Her hand accidentally goes to her belly. She looks down. I take her hand.

"Our daughter is doing really good," I say, and smile. I, too, am full of sadness.

This makes her happy. "I know. You tell me every time."

"I'm sorry. I forget when I leave this place."

"It's ok. I like hearing it every time. I need to hear it."

"Why are you here?" I ask.

"Where else am I supposed to be?" She asks like I should've known the answer all this time.

"Did I do this?"

Laura says nothing.

I think of my parent's death. The way they died in this life was exactly the same as in the other one. Why can't I have my mother here with us? Why do I have to be stuck with knowledge of the same death in two different worlds? Is it always meant to be this way? Is Laura always meant to be in the Red Plane? In my current life, my memories are only ashes in the wind, except Laura. Laura is my only link to a place I am supposed to forget, to only experience in dreams.

I stay a little longer; life is beautiful. There is beauty in such a sorrowful place, even in the charred and glistening buildings stretched out ahead of us. A storm is coming; I don't want Laura to experience it alone. I draw in close and wrap my arm around her. We watch as chaos unfolds; the only thing we are missing is soda and popcorn.

" I closed the door." I say, "I closed it to end the suffering."

"Yes," Laura says, "But there are other doors that will open."

There's a sun; there never was a sun in this world. It blinks. Something massive and writhing unfurls itself in the sky and descends upon the city below.

The End

About the Author

J.C. Walsh is a Rhode Island native now living in Philadelphia. As the saying goes, you can take the man out of Rhode Island, but he's going to take his monsters with him. A fan of Lovecraftian and cosmic horror, he plans to unleash his madness in the city of brotherly love, and gleefully watch as it spreads beyond. Having a love for horror movies, J.C. wrote articles about the genre for Scars Magazine, and then ventured on to self-published Blood Born Magazine that he and a friend created together. Now the things from beyond want to him focus on his writing, they want him to tell their story. If his supporting wife has survived the horrors for several years, maybe you will too after reading them. Maybe.

www.facebook.com/jcwalshauthor
www.twitter.com/jcwhorrorwriter
www.instagram.com/jcwalsh81

Made in the USA
Middletown, DE
13 April 2019